7

GHOST MINE

GHOST MINE

Steve Frazee

GUNSMOKE

First published in the US by Five Star

This hardback edition 2013
by AudioGO Ltd
by arrangement with
Golden West Literary Agency

ISBN 978 1 471 32153 5

British Library Cataloguing in Publication Data available.

Printed and bound in Great Britain by
TJ International Limited

Steve Frazee was born in Salida, Colorado, and for the decade 1926–1936 he worked in heavy construction and mining in his native state. He also managed to pay his way through Western State College in Gunnison, Colorado, from which in 1937 he graduated with a bachelor's degree in journalism. The same year he also married. He began making major contributions to the Western pulp magazines with stories set in the American West as well as a number of North-Western tales published in *Adventure*. Few can match his Western novels which are notable for their evocative, lyrical descriptions of the open range and the awesome power of natural forces and their effects on human efforts. *Cry Coyote* (1955) is memorable for its strong female protagonists who actually influence most of the major events and bring about the resolution of the central conflict in this story of wheat growers and expansionist cattlemen. *High Cage* (1957) concerns five miners and a woman snowbound at an isolated gold mine on top of Bulmer Peak in which the twin themes of the lust for gold and the struggle against the savagery of both the elements and human nature interplay with increasing, almost tormented intensity. *Bragg's Fancy Woman* (1966) concerns a free-spirited woman who is able to tame a family of thieves. *Rendezvous* (1958) ranks as one of the finest mountain man books and *The Way Through the Mountains* (1972) is a major historical novel. Not surprisingly, many of Frazee's novels have become major motion pictures. According to the second edition of *Twentieth Century Western Writers*, a Frazee story is possessed of 'flawless characterization, particularly when it involves the clash of human passions; believable dialogue; and the ability to create and sustain damp-palmed suspense.' His latest Western novel is *Hidden Gold* (1997).

Chapter One

SEVEN DAYS

The desk clerk at the Big Stope Hotel wore a
hard-boiled miner's safety hat and a miserable patch of blond
chin whiskers. His glance at the reversed register was fast and
casual, but he stumbled on the name. "How long will you be
with us, Mister . . . ah . . . Sadar?"

Rigdon Sadar's words were weighted evenly. "One week."

The clerk—Al Harris, according to the long pyramid of a
nameplate on the desk—reached sidewise for a record card,
looking at the long-fingered, powerful hand that had signed
the register. He threw a quick study on the lean, tanned face
of the rangy man across the desk. About six, four, Harris estimated, right around two hundred and ten. He began to write,
wondering about the intensity he'd seen in Sadar's dark-blue
eyes. "That's a fine beard, Mister Sadar. Mind telling me
how long it took?"

"Just a week," Sadar said. He might have been repeating
the answer to the first question.

*Sounds as if he had to flatten a mountain with a teaspoon in
that time*, Harris thought.

Sadar looked around the lobby, realizing for the first time
just how large the hotel must be. Three bulky columns down
the center of the room gave a realistic effect of unpulled pil-

lars in a mine stope. Everything in his life was tangled with mining. One week. Seven days that would telescope into each other with frightful speed. In that breath of time he had to find his way along an unblazed back trail, tangled and overgrown for forty-five long years. He had one week—no, only six days, considering that the present one was almost gone—to find and lay before the world a fortune in stolen gold.

There it is, people, twenty-seven sacks of calaverite. Take it, kick it around, fight over it—anything! But see it and leave me alone from now on. It's simple, Sadar reflected. *All I have to do is something that smart, determined men couldn't do in half a century. I find the gold, forget it, and a lot of other things are forgotten, too.* He imagined the incredulous smiles that would follow the public declaration that he intended to find one, maybe two, hundred thousand dollars' worth of high grade and walk away from it without so much as a souvenir. But that was just what he planned to do.

His life had been fouled with the taint of that calaverite long enough. Right now it was casting a nasty, sticky shadow on the forty thousand he had in clean money on the other side of the range, in his hometown. He needed that forty thousand to realize the mining dream he'd held for years, but he wasn't going to touch one cent of it until he had stilled all lies about its uncertain source.

He and Joe Tanner had planned their fluorspar deal a long time ago. It had taken Tanner all the war years and a little longer to clear title to the ground, and now he wasn't willing to wait on Sadar or anyone else longer than one week.

"Forget that old yarn about your grandfather stealing a pot of gold in Sylvanite," Tanner had said to Rigdon. "You saw him in Alaska during the war, and you know he made his dough up there mining, don't you? You're silly if you let ancient gossip get under your hide. I'm not waiting. It's taken five years for me to run down heirs and get that fluorspar property cleared so we can go ahead without getting tangled up in lawsuits about pay-off time. You're the guy that had the idea in the first place, and I always figured on you for a partner, but I'm not going to sit back and go blub-blub with my fingers across my lips while you suddenly get sensitive about where your dough came from. I say. . . ."

"Look, Tanner, you spent a lot of time and money to make sure there won't be any legal trouble about those claims in the future. I know that. But don't you think I want my future unencumbered, too? I've been fighting a lie all my life. At times I was silly enough to think it would die of old age . . . but it hasn't, and it won't. If I. . . ."

"You let that wild yarn get under your hide!"

Tanner was a right guy and his argument might be reasonable—unless Sadar looked back on a past that had included numberless fights at school; sly, bitter cracks every time he wore something new; and fighting those who could be fought or turning away from those who couldn't be silenced by direct action. Besides, Tanner's mother hadn't turned gray before her time and become a near recluse.

"Sure! Didn't you know? His grandfather swiped a million bucks from a mine somewhere. Then he skipped to Alaska and left behind his little girl. All these years he's been sending back little bits of that stolen money to his daughter and her boy."

Considering how strongly the lie had colored Sadar's life, he still didn't know much more of the truth than those who repeated the story without knowing *anything* of the truth. His mother had been grimly reticent to discuss the subject in his early years, trying to protect him, and tired of the whole affair by the time he had grown old enough to understand.

He did know that twenty-seven sacks of incredibly rich gold ore had disappeared from a mine in Sylvanite forty-five years before, and that his grandfather, Sam Rigdon, had left soon afterward for Alaska, leaving his motherless baby daughter, Emily, with relatives in a distant town. Four years later Sam Rigdon began to send large sums of money from Alaska. The lie about its source leaped to life at once, and it never died. Emily bore the abuse during her childhood, and, when she married, she and her husband stuck it out, too, refusing to run away. In spite of their troubles, the couple honored Emily's father by naming their son Rigdon. Rigdon was three when his father, Jonathan Sadar, was killed in a mine accident. Emily stayed in the same town, trying to outlive the old story, but she had underestimated the terrible velocity of a lie, and she had paid for that error by becoming bitter.

Rigdon wasn't bitter, but he'd had enough. While a ski trooper in Alaska during the war, he had visited his grandfather. Maybe he hadn't been tactful in abruptly charging into the problem that had colored his life, not fully appreciating that old Sam Rigdon must have suffered greatly himself from the lie as well. Grown gruff and touchy through years of self-imposed exile, old Sam had bristled like an enraged moose and waved toward the worked-out diggings that had produced his fortune.

"You damned young pup!" he had roared. "You're just like the rest of them idiots in the States who say I was a thief! What's the matter? Didn't I send you enough?"

Rigdon's temper had come off the bitts, and he had told his grandfather what he could do with his money. They had raged at each other, their minds meeting in mid-air like the heavy clash of claymores, neither realizing how much alike they were, until old Sam had said in a normal growl: "Shut up before I lose my temper." They had gotten along a little better after that, but Sam Rigdon refused to discuss the Sylvanite robbery.

"For years I soured my life over that," he had said. "Now I've almost forgotten it. I'm fixed so I can blow smoke at mosquitoes and tell everyone to go to hell, so don't ask me to scrape at old sores."

Nonetheless, Sam had produced settlement sheets for the ore mined at his Alaskan property over a thirty-five year period. Rigdon had sent back notarized copies of these documents to his mother, confident that the papers would prove the source of his grandfather's wealth, unaware that documentary evidence is the puniest of dams before the powerful sweep of a popular lie.

After the war Emily had pointed out a fact that had been growing in Rigdon's mind for some time: nothing but the calaverite itself would wither the tendrils of suspicion that had fastened themselves onto their lives. She told him that years before she had hired detectives to prove her father's innocence. Their report had been honest—the back trail was so cluttered with fallen years they could find nothing tangible to prove guilt or innocence. All they had come up with was the popular belief held by veteran miners in Sylvanite—the gold was still somewhere underground.

Tanner had been sympathetic but hard when Rigdon announced his decision to go to Sylvanite. He promised to hold the partnership open for one week. "One week is all, Rigdon. One year wouldn't be any greater help. I can guess how you feel, but you're riding at a windmill. For twenty or thirty years those mines have been dead. Damn it! Why don't you let people shake their tongues loose and come in with me while you got a chance?"

"I'm leaving today."

"You don't even know the details," Tanner had protested.

"I'll find them in Sylvanite."

He'd moved fast after that, not even taking time to shave the beard he'd grown for the Mining Roundup in his hometown. Tanner had flown him to Eldorado, fifty miles down the river from Sylvanite. Not wanting to wait overnight for the bus, Sadar had started hitchhiking, his third ride carrying him to the back door of the Big Stope in the cab of a farmer's truck loaded with manure and sacked potatoes.

Now, one day was almost gone. He felt the need for haste more strongly than ever, but he couldn't go rushing about wildly. Now he stood in the Big Stope, staring at the pillars, suddenly realizing with a mild shock that they were composed of skillfully joined granite. A lot of money had gone into remodeling the hotel, according to the farmer who had given him the lift into Sylvanite. "Trying to make a walloping dude center of the old camp, Rouvière is," the farmer had said. "Old P.T.F., as they call him, was a boy there when his uncle owned one of the rich mines. Rouvière's a millionaire on his own, though. Made it in real estate and construction in the East."

The clerk took in Sadar's broad back and tanned neck. Jackets, slacks, and open shirts weren't uncommon among Big Stope guests, but this fellow's apparel appeared to have been used for wearing, instead of display. Harris winked at two shock-headed bellhops in their early teens and leaned across the desk to look at Sadar's shoes. Although he didn't believe the advertisement he'd once read about shoes revealing a man's character, it still wouldn't do any harm to have a look. He discovered that Sadar's shoes were pretty big and dusty, but not bad. No, it was something in the set of the face, the purposeful way he had walked across the lobby, an intentness in his dark blue eyes that had marked him as different at first glance.

12

Harris's hard-boiled hat started to slip over his eyes. He pushed it back in place and grinned at the bellhops, who smiled wickedly. Each was wearing oversize pants held up by a single suspender.

Sadar watched the people streaming in and out of the big dining room. Sizing up the guests, he determined the hotel would be a poor place to start on his quest. He guessed he would have far better luck if he could meet and circulate among the old-timers. He turned. The bellhops reached for his bag at the same time, but one anticipated the other's move and shoved him backward.

Harris stifled a grin. "Here, you two! The Boom Days spirit isn't supposed to go any further than your clothes!"

"This guy looks like a good tip," said the victor as he swung the bag to one side and tried, too late, to keep the vanquished from snapping his suspender.

Harris grinned at Sadar. "*They* are part of the manager's idea of atmosphere during Boom Days," he explained. "The celebration starts at the end of this week."

Sadar grinned back at the desk clerk. "They'll do." He picked the victorious bellhop up by the seat of his pants and carried him, bag and all, toward the elevator.

Sadar's inside room was cooled and ventilated by a shaft outside the window. Water spilled irregular slaps down the masonry that caused air to move the new shade, tapping the ends of the stick that served as the weight at the bottom of the window shade against the casing. That shaft, Rigdon guessed, was probably original equipment. What with Sylvan Mountain outside and the mine atmosphere inside, he wouldn't be likely to forget why he was here.

He lathered in a shower with brand new plumbing, staring thoughtfully at a towel bearing the stope-like interior of the lobby in red stitching. "Free-spendin' manager up there," the farmer had said. "Between you and me, I sign a receipt for a little more than I actually get paid, but I get enough anyway."

Sadar considered shaving. The beard was a silly thing and itched a little under his chin. But it wouldn't be out of place with the celebration coming up, and it might prevent him from being recognized by some of the skiing crowd he knew. Even in summer one of that crowd might be hanging around the place.

He left the room and walked down the stairs, running one hand along the solid smoothness of gleaming mahogany. It felt good under his hand. Strong as a well-placed mine timber.

An orange-haired, buxom woman was standing near the bottom newel post. "Splendid, isn't it?" she asked. "To think that all this beautiful wood was *painted* over when Mister Rouvière bought the hotel!"

Sadar sized her up. The sort of woman who asked a question, smiled brightly while you tried to answer, and then speared in with her own answer or a story about her cousin before you had a chance to respond.

He went by fast, clicking his tongue. "Horrible thing! Awful!"

He paused before a mural that covered half of one long wall. Obviously reconstructed from a panoramic photograph, it gave a sweeping view of Sylvan Mountain and the mines in days long dead. Spenserian calligraphy on vellum behind glass in a gold leaf frame read:

No raw boom camp of crude shacks and tents was Sylvanite—but at its height a prosperous community where 10,000 owned homes of stable construction. At change of shifts, against

the black and silver of night, the lights of 5,000 miners made a glowing serpentine trail on Sylvan Mountain.

From the more than 500 miles of workings, abandoned since 1918, came fortunes that. . . .

Five hundred miles of drifts and stopes and raises. For thirty years the mountain had been crumbling inside. Spongy timbers mushroomed on the ends from the terrible pressure of creeping ground . . . acres of darkness below millions of tons of granite and quartzite. *A fine job you have,* Rigdon thought to himself. *One day gone, and you aren't even started.*

At the desk he asked: "Where do sensible citizens eat?"

The clerk had an unlighted miner's lamp on his hat now, and the weight seemed to be troubling him. He adjusted the hat and muttered: "Damn this Boom Days build-up." He glanced at the dining room. "Why . . ."—he grinned—"we eat at home."

Harris and Sadar smiled at each other like conspirators, Sadar realizing that he had found a liking for the desk clerk from the very first. He wondered how much Harris could tell him of Sam Rigdon's history in Sylvanite. The clerk might know the story, but he wasn't any older than Sadar, and his tale would be second-hand. No, the thing to do was get out among old-timers and then try to sort the facts out of some of the damnedest lies a man could hear.

"Our chow's good, but the price is strictly tourist," Harris said. "The Windlass Bucket, up the street four blocks, is the best I know."

"Thanks." Sadar turned to go and had to stop quickly to keep from colliding with a short, quick-striding man approaching the desk.

The man smiled, a full-blossomed action that ended as quickly as it began. "Sorry," he said, and went on to the desk. He was middle-aged, vigorously bald, and appeared to be hard-boiled and active. Slightly protuberant mild blue eyes belied the harsh expression of a square jaw and strong, hard lips. The lower half of the man's face gave Sadar the impression of a tough-tempered striking hammer.

"Hello, Mister Rouvière," Harris said. "How was your archery today?"

"Good form, poor score, Al."

Near one of the granite pillars Sadar rested his hands on the edge of a piece of heavy glass that covered a mineral display and tried to look interested in the specimens.

Rouvière was telling Harris that a bale of hay was no good to eat, even if you hit it dead center with an arrow. Sadar alternated between looking at the display of minerals and watching Rouvière. There was a man who probably could give him a great deal of straight dope about Sam Rigdon and the robbery. Rouvière had lived in Sylvanite when his uncle owned the mine. For a moment Sadar considered going directly to the millionaire and requesting an interview to explain his problem.

He watched Rouvière's face as the man turned his head to speak to a passing woman. The smile snapped on and off, relieving for just a wink the brutal flatness of the man's mouth and jaw. Sadar discarded his thought. Who in his right mind would credit Sadar's real motive in wanting to find the calaverite?

"What do you know? Maybe Sam Rigdon didn't get away with all that gold, after all. His grandson is in town looking for it. Of course, old Rigdon didn't tell him where to look!"

He scowled at a specimen resting on a shiny piece of fabric: **Calaverite from the Hibernian Mine**. All he

16

needed was twenty-seven sacks of that stuff. He allowed himself the cold-blooded thought that perhaps the high grade was long gone and that he was on a forlorn mission. It wasn't the first time he'd faced that possibility. Yet he had to move ahead.

At the desk the plump woman who abhorred painted mahogany—Mrs. Mahogany, he dubbed her from then on—was surrounding Rouvière. "You know," she said, "sometimes I don't believe people appreciate what you're doing here, Mister Rouvière. So often, in projects of this sort, the beautiful atmosphere of the past is ruined by some utterly incongruous modern atrocity!"

Like a shower room, Sadar thought. She ought to be forced to bathe in a wooden tub with water heated by hot rocks.

The woman began to warm up. Rouvière's smile blinked on and off politely, and he started to edge away.

"Now, if you could revive the former glory of the mines!" All Mrs. Mahogany needed to complete a heroic stance was a pick.

She's been moonstruck by the blush on that mural, Sadar thought.

"That would be a poor investment, I'm afraid," Rouvière responded.

He was looking straight at Sadar, but, even as Sadar stared back in an effort to determine whether the millionaire's glance was related to his words, Rouvière turned away, punched a polite excuse into the uncanny interval of silence while Mrs. Mahogany was switching fuel tanks, and made his escape.

Al became terribly busy with some cards, so Mrs. Mahogany eyed Sadar thoughtfully. He headed toward the street doors rapidly.

Relative distance assuring escape if pursued, he stopped

near the main entrance to look at a mining display. Four sets of posts and caps gave the wide doors the appearance of a mine portal. The framing, he noticed carefully, was strictly expert. Rusty picks and shovels leaned against the lagging; pieces of rock were scattered along the walls; a mine car sat on false rails just inside the lobby. He pushed gently against the box. It couldn't be budged. He saw, then, that some thoughtful soul had spot-welded the wheels to the axles. He grinned. A good thing, too, or those outlaw bellhops would be using the car to run down fat women in the lobby.

Both bellhops were outside, squatting by a dozen or more carbide lamps on the sidewalk. A slim girl, wearing silver-inlaid cowboy boots, was standing on a chromium barstool, hanging lamps on the spokes of a wagon wheel suspended from the marquee. Another girl in western gear was handing the lamps up. She smiled at Sadar.

"Look, Jackie, the Beard!"

The girl on the stool looked down and smiled. She wore tailored dungarees and a dark shirt that accentuated the blue of her eyes. Her hair was the color of a setter standing in sunshine on a bright October day. She was, Sadar decided instantly, an unusually good-looking girl.

"Tell me," she asked, "do you sleep with that beard under the covers or on top?"

"Come to think of it . . . ," Sadar began.

"He wears a snood on it," the second girl interjected, laughing loudly at her joke.

"I'll bet he keeps it in a traction splint," Jackie the girl on the stool opined.

"This lousy, damn' gasket leaks!" one of the shock-headed bellhops grumbled.

From above the girl's eyes lit with laughter. "Such language, Terry!" She looked at Sadar. "Give the boys a hand,

Beard. Terry and Gary, born under the sign of a bull in a china closet. Stout lads for atmosphere, though, about Boom Days time. Little do the guests know that Terry and Gary aren't acting!"

"Ah, Jackie," one of the bellhops moaned.

Sadar showed the bellhops the basic principle of hooking tanks to side pins before clamping the lamps together.

"That's easy," Terry or Gary grinned. "You a miner, chum?"

"Sort of," Sadar replied. He nodded toward the doors. "Who framed the timbers?"

"Old Deedee done that," one of the boys said.

"Deedee Ducray *did* that, Gary," corrected Jackie.

Sadar tucked the name away. Maybe this old Deedee was a miner. Still, anybody past eighteen was old to these kids, Sadar reminded himself.

Jackie rested one hand on his shoulder and jumped to the walk, stumbling slightly before she gained her footing. "Thanks," she said. "And don't mind our feeble cracks about your beard."

He grinned, catching a whiff of whisky as Jackie moved nearer and curtsied. "You're welcome."

He was turning to go, when a tall, wide-chested man approximately his own age stepped from the doorway. The fellow wore a short reddish beard, so thick each hair seemed to be clinched around another. The man scowled at Terry and Gary, who were tugging for the dubious honor of carrying the barstool. He measured Sadar with cold disapproval, then smiled at Jackie. His voice was smooth and careless when he said: "Did you forget you were going to have dinner with me, Jackie?"

"No, Biff," the girl said in the tone of one humoring an impatient child. She smiled at Sadar. "Thanks again."

The red-headed man gave Sadar a careless, insolent look. Sadar weighed him, and decided he didn't like him. He walked past the bellhops, who by now had compromised by sharing the barstool-carrying task, and started up the street.

Biff's voice followed him. "That fellow hitchhiked here on a load of fertilizer."

Sadar looked back. The girls, arms entwined, were stepping past Biff, who gave Sadar one last disapproving glance before following them into the hotel.

To hell with him, Sadar thought.

Chapter Two

DUDE BAIT

The present was thrusting up through the past in Sylvanite. Glass brick and travertine made up a gaudy bar front that stood between two rotting, sway-backed buildings where curled sheeting was skeleton gray beside broken, dust-dulled windows. Through gaps made by the wrecked buildings Sadar looked toward a back street and saw the stucco walls of small residences sitting between huge, windowless mansions. Over the carved top of Delmonico's Restaurant a wide clearing through the aspens on Sylvan Mountain marked a ski course that went up and up in sweeping curves, finally disappearing over the rounded summit. Beyond were blue-gray peaks, clean-limned against the evening sky.

Yesterday was lush, but today was lusty.

He stopped before an old man in khaki coveralls in front of a garage. Clean-shaved and sharp-eyed, the old fellow was sitting on a seat made of automobile cushions under a sign that said, **Ralston Motors, Inc.** He shifted as far as the upthrust coil springs, mushrooming out of the broken upholstery, would allow and eyed Sadar with a squint that was either fierce or questioning.

The old man shook his head briskly, when Sadar offered a cigarette, and squinted with obvious disapproval at the tall man's beard while Sadar was lighting up. The match *whirred* into the street and died.

"Where do you eat around here?" Sadar asked.

"Home." Sadar's beard was still getting a zero point zero inspection. "If'n I couldn't eat there, I'd leave town."

"That bad, eh?" Sadar glanced down the street. "Too bad Delmonico's isn't still running. That was really a restaurant, I hear!"

The old man relaxed a little. "You mean it was!" He began a fish-by-bird account of ancient menus, ending with the irrelevant challenge: "You ain't growing that beard for this here celebration, are you?"

Sadar said he wasn't.

Fifteen minutes later, after the old man had discovered that Sadar had been in Alaska, that Dutch Harbor, where the old-timer's grandson had been during the war, was not exactly on the Alaskan coast, that Sadar knew a stope wrench from a jim crow, his reticence dissolved entirely, and he offered half of his seat among the steel mushrooms. Sadar declined.

"Mines completely dead?" Sadar asked.

The old man spring-boarded off in the wrong direction. "Yep! Everything here is dude bait now. Ski course, paths to ride horses on . . . all that junk." He pushed a rusty spring, watched it pop up again. "Oh, that stuff brings in money, all right, but we got along right enough since the mines quit some good thirty years ago. We got a hospital, a damn' good grade school, fine county courthouse, our own power plant, and a lot of other things. We ain't asked nobody for nothing!" The old man spit explosively, then continued. "Then along comes this Reeves with Rouvière's money and gets everything stirred up. He gets a property boom started, gets folks to fighting each other bidding for lots and old buildings that nobody wanted a-tall a few years ago. Then he tells people what they ought to build and what to do and that they have to grow beards for this sucker celebration he cooked up. Why, hell!"

An automobile stopped before the pumps, and the driver yelled: "Hey, Charley! Where's your beard?"

Old Charley grinned and cursed good-naturedly and went toward the pumps. He looked back over his shoulder at Sadar. "Wait a minute, son, and I'll tell you some more."

"Gotta go, but I'll see you later," Sadar said. The way Charley had been steamed up, he probably wouldn't be able to talk about anything besides the local feud for some time.

Two blocks up the street Sadar saw a red neon sign flicker then steady into an outline that could pass for a windlass bucket. Beyond it, the huge sign on top of the Big Stope Hotel was lighted, but only the bright, spouting flames of the carbide lamps gave illumination at the entrance. He watched as two cars eased to the curb near the ball of light. Terry and Gary came running from the hotel.

Early dusk didn't soften the ruins that far out numbered the inhabitable structures, Sadar observed as he walked on. Night's pickets made sagging buildings more forlorn, wearier in their slow collapse. The new would win, the old was doomed, but let ancient ghosts die without interference. Let them crumble comfortably, he thought. Still, Rouvière had his side. The past was dead, and, if the natives fought each other in their greed over the new, that was because they were human beings, not because Rouvière inspired them to do so. He cut his speculations short. What Rouvière and his man Reeves were doing to the town was none of Sadar's problem, although he might have to listen to a lot of talk about their activities in the course of extracting information.

Under a fluted lamppost he stopped to drink the icy water spurting up from a green iron Mike in front of a drugstore where the curving legs of iron tables and chairs showed through the dusty windows. Overflow from the water fountain bubbled to a mossy basin for dogs at the base of the pedestal. His eyes narrowed when he read the small bronze marker on the fountain: **Presented to the City of Sylvanite by Mrs. Samuel T. Rigdon.**

A bald man in a white druggist's jacket came out from the store and sat down on an iron bench near the door. "Nice evening!" he hailed. "Up for the celebration?"

"In a way, yes." Sadar sat down beside the druggist. "Haven't seen a fountain like that for years. You know who was the woman was who gave it?"

"Oh, some civic-minded old battle-axe, I suppose."

Sadar edged around this unpromising start. "I've heard this used to be quite a town . . . rich mines, million dollar robberies, and so forth."

"Million dollar robberies?" The druggist considered. "Oh . . . that old vug story. I heard something about that when I first came here ten years ago, but you know how those tales are . . . hogwash and moonshine."

"I suppose." Ten-year resident, eh? Sadar lingered only long enough to confirm Harris's plug for the Windlass Bucket. The druggist added that Bob Reeves, Rouvière's manager, owned the Windlass Bucket.

Stagy, resplendent Western garb mingled with and made drab the working clothes of conservative citizens and the sports garments of tourists in the noisy crowded Windlass Bucket. To the mayhem and arson of a multi-colored juke box two young couples were cracking their joints in a weird dance. There was one vacant stool at the half horseshoe bar. Sadar took it. On his right was a moist-eyed woman whose caboose was putting a dangerous strain on her pale green slacks, on his left a morose, bitter-looking man about his own age was doodling with beer rings.

The woman on Sadar's right studied him covertly, then leaned to whisper to a chubby, bright-eyed girl companion. Both giggled and peered sidewise at Sadar. He turned to the sour lad on his left. Painfully clean-shaven, the fellow was hunched forward in a black leather jacket, absorbed with stale beer and a forefinger that showed the stubborn tracery of frequent dipping in grease and oil.

Sadar remembered the expert timber framing at the Big Stope.

"Do you know a man named Deedee?" he asked.

Something red-hot touched Sadar's cheek. He jerked toward the moist-eyed woman on his right. She was giggling. Clamped in small pliers were several brown whiskers from Sadar's face. She extracted one carefully with cardinal-enameled nails and held it toward the light. "Excellent, very excellent specimen, Myra," she told her companion.

"What the hell?" Sadar said.

Chubby Myra mined into a red plastic purse, producing a pencil and a sheet of paper that held several other hairs under Scotch tape. She leaned behind her companion to speak to Sadar. "Collecting. We bet a jeep against two saddle horses that we could go out and get more whiskers than two of our friends."

"It must have been a fine jeep," Sadar growled, rubbing his smarting cheek.

Myra's wide mouth was struggling hard to keep from smiling. "Name, please? Each and every specimen must be labeled in case of a spot check by the contestants."

"Cornelius J. Spook." Sadar glanced defensively around the room. Everyone seemed to be grinning except the bitter man on his left and a tall, elderly man in a new denim jumper.

The latter had one hand on a small glass of beer and was standing where the curving bar met the wall. He held Sadar's gaze a moment so fixedly that Sadar got the impression of startled intentness in the old man's eyes.

"C. J. Spook," Myra said slowly as she wrote. She leaned behind her companion and grinned at Sadar, an expression that was as impudent and friendly as her snub nose. "To show there's no hard feelings, I'll buy you a drink."

"Keep the whiskers, skip the drink."

"He's a grump, Myra," the second woman said. "Fine whisker grower, but a grump. C. J. Spook, Esquire, Grump."

The man on Sadar's left didn't lift his eyes from his tracings. "Damn' fool women!" he said in a harsh voice.

Sadar turned to him. "I can understand now why sensible people around here don't wear beards."

"Women grabbing whiskers isn't the reason. This whole beard business is a part of a build-up for the Boom Days racket!" The man's voice was savage, unnecessarily loud.

A youthful bartender, wearing luxuriant black sideburn whiskers, started to take Sadar's order, but digressed to give the bitter-faced man an angry look. "You tell 'em, Ralston! Everything Reeves does is a racket . . . since his boss turned you down on the Hibernian deal. But you don't get sore enough to quit robbing the tourists he brings in at that knocked-out joint you call a garage!"

"That's my business!" Ralston's face went the color of dirty gun metal. "You stick to mixing three cents' worth of whisky in six-bit drinks!"

The bartender laughed, winked at Sadar, and ignored Ralston who gulped at his beer and glared at the bartender. Ralston's green eyes didn't leave the youth when he shook his head curtly at Sadar's offer to buy.

The Hibernian—one of the calaverite specimens Sadar

had seen in the Big Stope had come from the Hibernian. He gave his order, and the bartender left.

"How long you worked the Hibernian?" Sadar asked.

"I never did work it," Ralston said brusquely. He looked contemptuously at Sadar's beard. "I see you fell in line with the edict the feudal lord got the mayor to sign."

"How's that?"

"Let your whiskers grow for Boom Days or get tossed in the clink and fined a couple of bucks!" Ralston's harsh voice filled the room in the interval while the juke box gasped for air and changed records. "What a racket! Where does the money go?"

A heavy-set, flushed youth with a fiery red beard risked a fall to lean far out on his stool and look at Ralston. "The sorehead grease jockey is wound up again!"

The juke box buckled down to murder and brimstone.

"I'm not bowing and scraping before the feudal lord, anyway!" Ralston shouted. "Rouvière and his stooge Reeves. They're even trying to call the ski course Rouvière Run!" Ralston's green eyes had an odd transparent look. His brown hair fell across his forehead. Lines running down from the corners of his nostrils deepened.

He works up quite a lather, Sadar thought, *and generates enough steam to blow his top when the pressure gets too heavy.* Sadar noticed that the old man in the denim jumper was watching Ralston quietly.

"Who built the damn' ski course in the first place?" Ralston demanded.

The woman next to Sadar said: "You . . . with your little red hatchet, Jackie boy."

In an undertone the woman named Myra warned her friend: "Don't needle him."

Ralston's face twisted. "By God! I helped the sportsmen's

27

club build most of that course six years before Rouvière came slumming in the old hometown and *discovered* what a wonderful skiing country this is!"

"Stow that stuff, loudmouth!" The lad with the fire-red beard, leaning out again, almost fell off his stool.

"When I get ready, I will!" Ralston shouted.

"I'll help you get ready!" The beefy youth lurched off his stool and came staggering along the bar. Two women in cowgirl outfits tried to stop him.

"Outside with it!" the bartender shouted.

"Let him come on!" Ralston yelled.

Beautiful luck, Sadar thought. *After rolling snake eyes twice, I finally find a guy who might want to re-open an old mine for the same reason I'm here, but he has to be a bastard and start a brawl. He ought to lose teeth for being offensive.* But there was something resigned and pitiful in the fear that underlaid Ralston's defiance and anger. Something that said: This is an old story, but I can't help it.

Sadar got off his seat and waited for the oncoming drunk, who was momentarily delayed by having fallen sideways between two seated customers. He recovered, pushing himself from the bar so forcefully he almost fell the other way. He flung aside the two women trying to stop him and came on.

At the curve of the bar, the denim-covered arm that shot toward the drunken youth's shoulder had a big hand on the end of it, a hand that stopped the lad so abruptly one foot went forward and his head snapped back. "Easy, son," the old man said. "Want to wreck the joint, lose your job, and get jugged for a month?"

After a foggy process that might have been thinking, the lad said he guessed he didn't. His belligerence faded into stupid bewilderment, and he let the synthetic cowgirls lead him back to his seat, where, after one drink and some reflection that may have touched upon the fact that, somehow, he had been frustrated in something, he began an insane, loud argument with the bartender.

The old man came up to Ralston and Sadar. "Jack," he said to Ralston, "somebody that don't know you may lower the boom on your sometime." He looked with frank interest at Sadar. "Who's your friend, Jack?"

"Him? He . . . hell, I don't know!" Ralston scowled at Sadar. "You started to ask about Deedee Ducray a minute ago. Well, here he is."

Sadar introduced himself to both men. Ralston's handshake had all the vigor of a dead trout. But there was hardness and power in the big, square-tipped hand Ducray thrust forward. He was bigger than Sadar had first thought, wide-shouldered, with plenty of meat apparent under the shiny new jumper. Somewhere in his early sixties, Sadar thought, his age showing most in the slight sag of flesh away from high cheek bones and jaw angle. Thick, coarse gray hair lay like a cap on Ducray's skull; his eyes were lively, brown, hooded at the outside corners; his nose was big and jutted like a sail.

Sadar grinned. "I saw your timbering at the hotel. Mighty nice framing, I'd say."

"Thanks. Not many kids your age would know that." Ducray gave Sadar's beard the once-over. "You live around this part of the mountains?"

"I came to Alpine from Washington last year." The truth was a lie, but let it be. "You an old-timer here?"

Ducray nodded. "Born in Sylvanite. Know its history like a book."

There's the opening you've been waiting for, Sadar told himself. *This guy is tailored to order, and he's standing right here with a* your move *look in his eye.*

29

"I'm interested in spar property," Sadar said. "Fluorspar mainly. Any here?"

Ralston snorted. "Damn' little!"

"There's some spotty deposits down the valley," Ducray said. "Never been any development work that I know of."

The bartender delivered Sadar's drink. Ralston and Ducray declined his invitation to have one. He took a slow drink, mentally agreeing with Ralston's crack about three cents' worth of whisky. Then he looked at the pair and invited both to have dinner with him.

Ralston shook his head. "I got work."

Ducray looked at the booths along the wall. "I know where we can get some real grub."

Sadar tossed a dollar on the bar. "Lead on."

Ralston walked outside with them. He grunted what might have been—"Good night." or "Go to hell!"—and walked down the street, a lean, thin-chested figure with a chip-on-his-shoulder stride. Sadar watched him go and smiled. "Don't tread on me."

"He's all right," Ducray said. "His disposition is not his fault, and he just don't like Reeves a little louder than some of the rest of us."

"The bartender claimed it was over a mine deal."

Ducray laughed. "That may be. Ralston owns the Hibernian . . . inherited it. There's talk that he tried to get Rouvière to finance a re-opening." He started up the street. "It's quite a little walk where we're going." After several paces he said: "The Hibernian and the Vivandière lie side by side."

Vivandière, eh? Sadar thought. *I'm supposed to recognize the name.*

Ducray led him toward a section of town where no lights showed among the ruins. Sadar raised his eyes to dark Sylvan

Mountain. Perhaps somewhere deep under that dark coat of aspens lay twenty-seven sacks of calaverite; somewhere in the gloom and water that had been accumulating for thirty years; somewhere a pile of high grade layered by rotted canvas . . . five hundred miles of workings. . . .

"The old holes caved pretty bad?" he asked.

Ducray gave him a quick glance. "Some parts had awful bad runs that was spiled. In those places the whole country would be down now. Then there's drifts where the granite is probably solid as a church today. On top the hill I got a little penny-ante hole, but that's the only place that Mister Dupont had been burnt in many's the long year."

"Any of the mines go for taxes . . . like the rest of the property everybody's been scrambling to buy up?"

"Not none of the big ones, like the Hibernian and the Vivandière. Rouvière owns the Viv . . . inherited it from his uncle, old Marcus Besse. All the big producers are still owned by somebody paying taxes. People just naturally hang on to old holes." They walked on in silence.

Nothing was inadequate about the lighting system of Sylvanite, Sadar noticed. Even on deserted streets each corner had a lamp. Brick structures showed now and then among the ruins of less substantial buildings; the walks were made of honest concrete; the streets were wide and well-drained.

As they stepped from a high curb at an intersection, Ducray grunted and grabbed Sadar's shoulder. The old man nearly fell before Sadar could get an arm around him.

"Down. Let me sit down a minute," Ducray muttered.

Sadar helped him to a sitting position on the curb. Ducray leaned sidewise and stretched out one leg. His face was gray.

"Heart?" Sadar asked.

Ducray shook his head. "Trick hip from a cave-in when I

was younger than you." He leaned to the side on one arm and worked his right leg. "Sometimes just a little step the wrong way makes my back and hip feel like the way they was that night I come into the hospital."

Several minutes later Sadar helped him rise. Ducray's face was still pale, covered with fine sweat. "I'll be all right now. You didn't think I was going to die, with supper just around the corner?" His laugh was game, and he limped on.

Chapter Three

THE FIRE HOUSE BOYS

The light they neared came through clean windows in a narrow, two-story building. It shone defiantly amidst the somnolent ruins in the deserted street, as if daring the dead past to shoulder too hard against this lone building.

Inside, a massive mahogany bar and an ornate, carved back-bar ran almost the entire length of a narrow room, ending just short of wide doors that opened the side wall. The place was brightly lighted by a number of bare bulbs on drop cords running down from a metal ceiling. The entire wall opposite the bar was covered with framed pictures. At the end of the room was one narrow door.

The man behind the bar near the wide doors didn't move when Sadar and Ducray entered. His face was toward them, with light from the bulb above him making the dead center part of his black hair look like a long scar.

Sadar and Ducray went forward, passing a long table with eight heavy chairs. It seemed to Sadar that he was walking straight into the past toward an uncertain goal.

The man behind the bar continued to stare, not speaking. He was of Ducray's age, Sadar estimated, shorter and powerfully stacked. No trace of gray showed in the thick black hair that, in addition to being parted in the middle, curled back from the temples in the mode of bartenders that Sadar had never seen, save in pictures. For a moment Sadar thought he'd seen surprise on the man's face, but, as he came closer and looked into hard slate eyes, he could read nothing but impassiveness on the wide, brown face.

From somewhere beyond the wide doorway at the end of the bar Sadar heard the *clink* of poker chips.

"What's your name, lad?" the man behind the bar asked suddenly. His voice carried a sepulchral boom, his words coming forth like the measured thump of thick liquid from a stone jug.

Ducray spoke up and introduced the two. "This is Ben Liggett," he told Sadar. "He's sort of the shift boss at the Fire Horse Club here. A few of us old-timers that don't think much of the new deal in Sylvanite try to stick together the best way we can."

Ben's brown-mottled hand was warm and heavy. His grip, Sadar decided, didn't come from tending bar.

"Brought the boy over to eat," Ducray explained.

"Where you from, son?" Ben asked.

"Alpine."

Ben nodded slowly. He studied Sadar closely for several minutes then moved one hand behind the bar. A switch clicked.

"Lived in Alpine long?" Ducray asked.

Sadar was looking across the room at a large picture of a boxer. "I've been there since I came from Washington." He pointed with his head. "Who's the fighter?"

"Jack Dempsey," Ducray said. "The original Jack Dempsey, the Nonpareil."

Sadar walked across the room. Old Jack Dempsey was in good company there on the wall—Sullivan, looking ready to curse; Corbett, his hair neatly combed; bald-headed old Fritz

Choynski; Tom Sharkey, the Durable Dane.

Ben was moving utensils behind the bar, humming the "Monterey Waltz" in a voice that was occasionally sonorous, but mostly rumble. Ducray limped to the table and sat down.

Sadar moved down the hall. Here was a panorama of Sylvanite in the early days, doubtless a print of the same picture from which the mural in the Big Stope had been copied. He looked at the images—hose cart teams, muscular lads with lots of hair, bare chests, and baggy tights. Before he glanced at the name he knew the big, smiling, bearded man standing by a hose cart.

Samuel T. Rigdon, Team Captain
World's Championship Hose Cart Team
from Vivandière Mine.
Leadville Competition, July 4th, 1897.

"Those pictures are almost relics now," Ducray commented, chuckling to himself. "You don't know how bad Reeves wanted to buy everything in this saloon. We barely beat him to it."

Sadar turned from the wall. "I can see how everything would fit into the old-time atmosphere Rouvière is trying to revive." He glanced toward the wide doors, listening to the sounds of cards and chips.

"Take a look at the casino," Liggett suggested.

Ducray rose. "I'll show you. My hip gets better faster if I walk on it, anyway."

Five old men were playing poker under a bright light at a round table in a room so large more than half of it was lost in shadows. From what Sadar could see, it appeared that all the saloon's original equipment was stacked somewhere in this room.

One man in an undented black hat that shadowed his eyes

was watching the game. His head jerked nervously toward Sadar when he entered the casino.

"Boys, this is Mister Sadar," announced Ducray.

The poker players looked up indifferently. Two or three muttered howdy, then turned back to the game. In that instant's break Sadar saw the man, who was getting ready to deal, cut the cards twice with one hand while both hand and deck were clear of the table. It was an old trick Sadar had practiced himself for amusement during long days in Alaska, but he'd never been able to accomplish it twice in a row without spilling the cards.

He appraised the dealer. The fellow wore a rumpled white shirt, flowered tie askew at the collar, and a shapeless brown suit. His fine, thin gray hair stuck up in disorderly wisps; his eyes were small, close-set and full of humor, and his face broad and red. He could easily imagine him in overalls behind a plow.

"Play 'em like you had 'em!" the dealer said jovially. Blunt, clumsy-looking fingers completed the deal. He looked at Sadar and grinned.

There is an artist, Sadar thought. *I'll bet he dealt seconds all the* way, *and I couldn't even hear it.* He recalled smooth, likable Angelo Griego, two years a soldier in Alaska by request, professional gambler by choice. Angelo had spent many an evening in the Quonset, showing Sadar every crooked card trick he knew—and Angelo had known plenty. But this dealer—Swede, he must be, by accent and appearance—could make Angelo look stiff-fingered and clumsy on that cut trick alone. A man who could cut that little dido with the smooth, noiseless speed the dealer had shown could probably do anything with cards.

He looked around the table. All five men had plenty of chips.

Two men stayed with the Swede when he opened. They drew cards, bet freely, and stood on the Swede's raises, hiking the bets until pale yellow chips lay spilled like wafers of gold in the center of the table. The cards went up, and the dealer pawed the pot toward him with blunt, awkward-looking hands.

"Well! I sure am lucky!" he guffawed.

You sure are, Sadar thought.

He felt Ducray's hand tap his side, and turned. One of the players, a small man in a black hat, was standing several feet away, peering intently into Sadar's face. The man's eyes flashed restlessly, played over Sadar's countenance like points of steel.

"Meet Sim Tarwater," Ducray said. "Sim used to be a night shifter on the Vivandière."

The little man shot Ducray a startled look. He edged closer to shake hands, his manner implying that he was going to get the job done and then leap back to safety.

Tarwater's grip was talon-like, all the pressure coming from his thumb and forefinger. Sadar glanced at the hand as Tarwater withdrew it. The knuckles showed craters like black scars on an aspen trunk; running from under the tight clasp of a black jersey sleeve, the white-ridged scar of a brutal injury angled across the back of the small hand. Small wonder three of the man's fingers were half curled and stiff.

"Sadar, huh?" Tarwater's voice was low, calm, and bore a strange soothing quality that was in hard contrast to the leaping, disturbed expression of his eyes. They weren't black, Sadar decided. Dark blue made darker by the color of his hat and the black Navy jersey. His thin coppery face was hatchet-like, his mouth full-lipped and composed. Only the darting play of his eyes indicated inner tension.

"That's right," Sadar said.

"I don't remember that name, but. . . ." Tarwater's eyes flicked over Sadar's beard and went questioningly to Ducray. "You look all right to me." He went quickly back to his position.

The Swede lost three pots in a row to three different players, and laughed loudly at each loss.

Little Sim Tarwater kept darting worried glances at Sadar.

From the wide doorway Liggett's voice boomed. "Grub is ready!"

I wonder how that voice would sound in a big, empty building at night? Sadar asked himself.

As he passed the end of the bar, he saw a squat refrigerator, an electric stove, and a gleaming sink behind the wide mahogany. The Fire Horse boys were doing all right. He wondered where their money was coming from. On the bar, sizzling in a huge blue platter with Dutch windmills, was the biggest steak Sadar had seen in a long time. Liggett was setting out more dishes.

Sadar and Ducray carried the food to the long table.

A half hour later Sadar said: "That was as big as a moose steak and not half as lean. I'd say you boys hadn't suffered, bucking Rouvière."

Ducray prodded at his teeth with the nail of his little finger. "We're against Reeves, but, mainly, we're against being bought body and soul. That's what'll happen here, if he has his way. A lot of the old-timers here ain't eaten so good at times, but they've always been independent. Some of us want to stay that way. Sure, we'll take Reeves's money when we can get it. I got a right fair wad for framing those timbers you saw, but so far all he's bought from most of us is our labor."

Sadar could see that Ducray was following the general line. Reeves's policies in the application of Rouvière's wealth were the major points of resentment, not the millionaire himself or his plans, except as Reeves made them distasteful.

Ducray's brown eyes were earnest. "Let me tell you a little. Reeves is a local boy. He got around quite a bit in the newspaper business . . . correspondent during the war and all of that. Somewhere he got acquainted with Rouvière, and together they hatched up this plan of bringing the town back. . . ."

Sadar nodded. "I see." He wondered if Ducray would later pursue that stall about fluorspar. It hadn't been a very good lie in the first place, and the old man must have recognized it as such. No, it looked apparent that Ducray's motive in bringing him to the Fire Horse had been something else. He listened with half attention to Ducray's version of the local feud, wondering how he could get the subject back to more important matters.

". . . something to help the town along. So Reeves got a Hungarian or Romanian, or something, to make a survey about finding handicraft work for the natives here to help themselves. This lousy foreigner compared Sylvanite to some little village in Europe where the peasants were saved from starvation by making sheepherder's cloaks or capes of some kind for export to this country." Ducray shook his head bitterly. "When that story come out in a Denver paper, it made us look like a bunch of hungry, ragged peons. That's just one of the cock-eyed things Reeves done around here. How would you feel?"

"Pretty damned sore." Sadar wasn't inattentive now. Reeves must be an arrogant bastard for sure.

Ducray had draped his denim jumper over the back of his chair. Sadar saw that the old man's shirt was worn and patched. All the bottles on the back-bar, he'd noted before, were empty as a second lieutenant's head. Still, there was expensive equipment behind the bar, that stove and all. The poker players had been betting heavy, even if it was just a penny ante game.

"Rouvière has brought money into the town, hasn't he?" Sadar asked.

"No argument there. It's just the way Reeves has gone about things that galls us."

"How about Rouvière?"

"He ain't been here much till this summer. He's left things pretty much up to Reeves."

Sadar looked at the display of empty bottles across the room. Ben Liggett was standing at the bar, his thick forearms crossed and leaning on the wood, his face a big brown blot as he stood quietly and listened.

"How do you keep this place going?" Sadar asked. "You don't serve meals or drinks here regularly, do you?"

"We were going to run the bar, but Reeves blocked us from getting a city license," Ducray explained. The corners of his eyes seemed more hooded than ever. "Oh, we do one thing and another." He glanced toward the casino and grinned to himself. "Take that little fraction I got on top the hill. It never was patented and was sort of overlooked for years. Ben and me accidentally staked it just before Reeves decided to run the ski course another three thousand feet along the top of the mountain." He grinned like a pirate. "Of course, it cost him a little to cross our ground. Then we had a little dumb luck and ran into a narrow streak of high grade. It helps out some." Ducray was then silent for a long time.

Sadar decided to plunge into his calaverite hunt. "Tarwater was a shifter on the Vivandière in the old days, you said?"

Ducray nodded slowly, his eyes hard on Sadar's face. "He was there when the vug was robbed."

"That was the million dollar job, eh?"

"Not by a long swipe! But it was plenty . . . twenty-seven sacks of damn' rich calaverite went out of a vug with a bank vault door on it . . . went out of a back door that wasn't supposed to be there. It didn't go far, though. It's still in the hill."

"How do you know?"

"It didn't get out of the hill the night it was took because the regular dry-room checks made it tough for a man to get out with a piece of high grade big as a pea, let alone twenty-seven sacks of anything. From the day after it was stole, there was a man or two from the mine owners' association at every hole that was even close to the Vivandière Number Four. From then on, there's a lot of good reasons why that calaverite never came to sunlight." Ducray leaned forward. "She's there yet, and it would cost a man more than the stuff is worth to get at it . . . even if a man knew where it was. There she is and there she'll stay, long after both of us are gone."

Sadar wondered if Ducray's positiveness was a calculated effort to discourage. If it was, that meant Ducray knew why Sadar was in Sylvanite, knew who he was. The longer he considered the possibility, the surer Sadar became that he was right. For one thing, Ducray's story of the robbery had been rather incomplete, as if the teller assumed the listener knew a great many details already. Nonetheless, he didn't get a chance to select any one of the questions jarring against others in his mind.

Car lights swept against the windows, then steadied in a blaze against the front of the building that threw reflection back into a maroon convertible with the top down. Two couples got out of the automobile. A cub bear tried to follow and almost threw itself as its chain came up short against its mooring on the steering post.

"There's Jackie Rouvière," Ducray said, and, shaking his

head, he added: "and she's in damn' poor company again."
He called across the room to Liggett. "Get Reeves's bid up as
high as you can . . . and then we'll harpoon him some more to
see him wiggle." To Sadar he explained: "Reeves would like
to buy our casino loot for his damn' poker festival during
Boom Days. We've been stringing him along."

"We're stringing him only till he gets right on the bid,"
Liggett growled. "This place don't run on air, Deedee." He
cleared his throat with a sound like the drive of a shovel into a
coal pile.

"He won't get right," opined Ducray.

The first girl inside, accompanied by a long-jawed, balding
young man wearing glasses, was the Myra who had connived
in pulling the hairs from Sadar's beard. When she saw him, she
grinned instantly. She simulated a fiendish look and made
plucking motions with her fingers against her cheek.

In spite of himself, Sadar grinned in return. He was not surprised to see that Jackie Rouvière was the same Jackie who had
been hanging lamps when he had come out of the hotel. The
big, swagger-chested, red-bearded man with her was the same
fellow who had given Sadar the insolent look from the Big
Stope doorway—Reeves. He tried to classify Jackie Rouvière
according to how much she might know of her father's knowledge of the Vivandière mine, but his mind went astray.

The four started up the narrow room. But Myra and her
escort diverged to look at the photos lining the wall. Reeves
and Jackie came on. He was holding her arm as if dragging
her through a crowded railroad station. He didn't give Sadar
a retake. The first glance was thorough and seemed to indi-
cate that he considered Ducray and Sadar fitting company for
each other, but his voice was smooth when he said: "Good
evening, Deedee."

Ducray nodded.

Abreast of the long table, Jackie halted and tapped her arm. "May I have this back now?"

"Oh!" Reeves smiled agreeably. "I didn't realize. Excuse me a minute while I talk to Ben." He went up to Liggett, who didn't bother to grunt in reply to a pleasant salutation.

Jackie came directly to the table. "Don't get up," she said to Sadar and Ducray, even though both men had already gained their feet. Ducray's face was proof that, if he didn't like Rouvière, the animosity didn't include Rouvière's daughter. He stumbled a little in introducing Sadar to her.

"We met, more or less, at the hotel this evening," Jackie said.

Some of his age seemed to leave Ducray as he beamed at the girl. *I'll bet that old duck got around in his day,* Sadar noted.

"In my day we couldn't meet young women so easy-like," Ducray said. "That whistling stuff would've got us what-for!"

"He didn't whistle, Deedee."

"What did he do, then?"

"I used the fluorspar gag," Sadar said, watching Ducray intently.

The old man's quick smile showed Sadar what he'd suspected—Ducray hadn't been taken in for a second by the lie. Probably Ralston hadn't, either.

"Deal me in," Jackie said. "Or is this some of that rugged *man* talk?"

"I just lied a little about being a spar promoter in order to crash a good place to eat," Sadar teased.

Jackie smiled. "I wondered what you were doing in this nest of opposition to light and progress. At first, I thought you were somebody Biff had imported for color . . . that is, until I saw him check your name with Al Harris."

Sadar knew he did a poor job of concealing surprise.

"He was disturbed that a guest of the Big Stope should arrive on such an . . . an unusual cargo." Jackie's tone implied that she was needling both Reeves and Sadar.

Sadar looked at Ducray. "I came in with a farmer hauling fertilizer and spuds." He felt the need for further explanation and was irritated by it. "I didn't want to wait for a bus in that place down the river." He regretted the unnecessary clarification instantly.

Ducray laughed and said: "Well, it got you here, didn't it?" and Jackie added: "That bus *is* no bargain."

Sadar saw the unspoken question that both held silent, and thought: *Yeah, and now both of you are asking yourselves why I was in such a hurry.* His eyes traveled to Ducray's face.

The old man was studying him carefully.

Jackie sensed something in the exchange of looks between the two men. "I don't want to interrupt a big mining deal or something," she said, "so I'll just pop over and look at the art gallery. This is the first time I've ever been in this rebel stronghold for a long time, you know, Deedee. Before I start the tour, I want to know who that man threatening his wife is." She looked toward the back-bar where a mirror had been removed to hang a large picture of a slender man jabbing a belligerent finger and holding a chair in one hand.

Ducray chuckled. "That's Billy Sunday. He's just before busting the devil and demon rum with that chair."

"When that picture was hung, I imagine he couldn't have found a better place than this to campaign," she said. She walked toward the couple that had worked down to the hose cart pictures by now. Looking back at the bar, she said: "Ben, if you can rustle up a bottle, I'll take a double of whatever you got."

Ducray tipped his head and watched her go. "She don't look or act a bit like her old man."

"Just a little around the eyes, only his sort of pop out," Sadar said.

Ducray regarded him quietly. "You know Rouvière?"

Sadar shook his head. "I saw him, that's all."

They sat down again, and unspoken matters they had been probing toward carefully came back strongly in their minds.

Between laughs of the foursome studying the photographs, sounds of the poker game drifted in from the casino. Little Sim Tarwater peered around the casing for an instant, then withdrew like a shy animal. Tarwater, Sadar had decided, would be the very man to talk to about the Vivandière robbery. Ben Liggett leaned in monolithic calm on the bar while Reeves enumerated the various reasons why the gambling equipment stacked in the Fire Horse casino should not be allowed to lie unused. Ben seemed unimpressed.

"It's the most complete lay-out of old-time gambling equipment I ever saw," Reeves explained enthusiastically.

"I know that," Ben rumbled.

"How does this sound?" Reeves made an offer.

"Not near good enough."

"The stuff is doing no good where it is," Reeves pursued.

"That's right."

Reeves's voice did not rise, but exasperation began to soak into his tone. "Why be a dog in a manger?"

"Why be a cheap-skate?"

Sadar saw the back of Reeves's neck redden.

"See here, Ben, I'm only trying to help you fellows along, even if you are the worst die-hard bloc I've had to contend with in Sylvanite."

"I know." Ben's utter detachment was enough to irritate a saint.

Ducray was grinning hugely.

Sadar's eyes strayed toward Jackie. He decided he liked

the way she moved, the way she held her head when she smiled. *A millionaire's daughter, eh?* he pondered. *Don't get any ideas*, Rigdon. *You've got a big enough job on your hands as it is. Still, a man could look, couldn't he? No law against that.*

"See here, Deedee," Reeves said, turning his attention to Ducray, "what do you think about that equipment in the casino? You and Ben own it jointly, don't you?" He had crossed the room while asking the question and was standing by the table now. His voice was level, but there was tightness in his eyes that betrayed his irritation.

"Why, I think it's pretty good stuff," Ducray evaded.

Sadar grinned and was rewarded with a mind-your-business stare from Reeves. He wanted to tell Reeves to go to hell. He knew he had taken an anti-Reeves position from the minute old Charley had begun to tell about the feud. On top of that, his dislike for Reeves had begun from his first glimpse of the man. Although he realized that even mental involvement in the local difficulty was a bootless detour away from his goal, Sadar couldn't help himself. He widened his grin and watched Reeves's face.

"You know what I mean," Reeves told Ducray. "I've given you fellows a lot of work, Ducray. I've bought your damn' vegetables, and. . . ."

The old man began to bristle. His lips tightened, and his eyes blazed. "Sure you have! Now you want us to *give* you that gambling equipment so you can rob each and every tourist sucker all during Boom Days!"

"That's not exactly accurate, Deedee." Reeves's eyes were tight with anger, but his voice was still controlled.

"Call me a liar!" Ducray leaped up. He grabbed Reeves's arm.

Startled, Sadar thought how unlike the man's previous behavior this action was. He looked at the big hand on Reeves's

forearm, and remembered how easily it had stopped the beefy
drunk who was going for Ralston. He heard Jackie call: "Biff!
Deedee! Don't be fools!"

"I didn't call you a liar . . . exactly." Reeves started to de-
tach the hand from his arm. "Now take it easy, Pop."

"Don't you Pop me, you young punk!" Ducray raised his
other hand.

Reeves stepped back, at the same time jerking his arm free
and pushing the old man away. It was not a vicious shove, but
Ducray staggered backward. His face went gray, and he
dropped into his chair with a groan. "Damned hip!" he muttered savagely.

Sadar didn't push his chair back, but rose swiftly, slicing
his legs between the chair and the table. He faced Reeves.
"You don't do bad with old people, Reeves."

"It's none of your business, Sadar." Reeves's eyes were
hard and watchful. "You stick to your fertilizer hauling. And
be sure you have the money for your hotel bill at the end of
the week."

Even as he jabbed his left hand out, Sadar realized Reeves
had been waiting for that very feint. The red-bearded man
moved his head easily. He beat Sadar's right by a fraction,
and Sadar stumbled backward across the narrow room. His
cheek bone felt numb, and the back of his head was aching. If
he hadn't managed to get his nose to one side of that one. . . .
His head hit the bar. One foot was still moving. It became entangled between the bar and brass rail.

"For heaven's sake, Biff!" Jackie sounded disgusted.

Big and solid in the middle of the narrow room, Reeves
looked at the girl and smiled. "He asked for it."

Sadar's efforts to free his foot seemed frenzied. He
threshed around like a horse hobbled for the first time. He
half stumbled when he left the bar, charging straight toward

Reeves. The red-bearded man's smile turned to a sneer. He shifted his feet a little and waited. Sadar's right hand was low and cocked as if poised for a mighty, up curving roundhouse. He started the swing.

Reeves's timing was almost perfect. Sadar's momentum should have provided half the force to leave him flat on the back of his neck after the other's fist came through. The blow came through all right, but Sadar's head wasn't there. He'd checked his wild rush and was leaning back when Reeves's straight right flashed at his chin. Sadar went under the arm and struck twice just below Reeves's breast bone. The red-bearded man's knees and hips twisted with the blows. His big wrists were straight.

Reeves's cough was a gush. He doubled over, and his knees started to unhinge. Sadar straightened him with a short uppercut. Then he drove his shoulder into the man's stomach and grasped him behind the knees. Reeves was almost limp when Sadar came erect with him in a flour-sack carry and started for the door. Myra's long-jawed date with glasses opened the door.

Sadar dumped his burden on the sidewalk in a sitting position. Reeves's legs weren't in good working order yet, and he was having a little trouble getting air. He gasped and gave Sadar a look of bitter, burning hatred. "This . . . isn't over. Let me . . . catch . . . my . . . breath."

"That's enough for one session," Jackie said. She stood before Sadar for a moment, studied his beard, ran her eyes over his face as if wanting to be sure of something.

"He asked for it," Sadar said, watching Jackie carefully.

Jackie nodded calmly, her eyes wide and dark. "So he did."

Chapter Four

THE THIRD WARNING

Sadar heard the maroon convertible pulling away before he reached the table on his return to the saloon. Ducray was sitting on the floor, leaning sidewise and working his leg. Some of the poker players were standing around him. Ben Liggett hadn't moved from the bar. His arms were still folded before him, and his brown face was inscrutable.

Sadar felt his cheek bone, decided it was cut enough so he might not have a mouse. He felt let-down, disgusted with himself. He looked at Ducray. The poker players still stood impotently, not touching him. Apparently they had not seen his trick hip in action before. Light gleamed on Ben's black hair, blazing on the center part as he continued to lean on the bar.

Damn such exercise right after chow, Sadar reflected. *It makes a man's food lay on his stomach like an old rubber boot.* He eyed Ducray narrowly. "Did you promote that thing purposely?" Sadar asked.

Ducray twisted his head and grinned with white lips. His face was the color of his smooth cap of gray hair. That and his pain-darkened eyes gave him a death's head look. "You didn't think I was fool enough to tackle a big youngster like him on my own?"

Ben's mausoleum voice boomed out. "Help him in to that extra bed in my room."

Ducray shook off hands and got to his feet by himself. He didn't protest when, after a few dragging steps, two men helped him through the narrow door at the back of the room.

Sadar looked around for Sim Tarwater. Obviously Sim hadn't come from the casino to see the fight. Neither was the Swede present. Sadar went along the bar and looked inside the casino. The Swede was sitting alone at the card table, idly looking at his hands. He looked up and grinned. "Short fight, lad. It was over before I could get started."

Little Sim Tarwater was gone. The poker players walked past Sadar as he stood in the doorway. One of the pair who had helped Ducray into the bedroom grumbled to his companion as they went by: "Ain't that Deedee the damnedest one to growl at you when you try to help him?"

Sadar turned just as Ben took his arms from the bar and started to stow a Frontier Model Colt that had been lying behind his heavy wrists. "Just in case that salmon-jawed fellow got gay," he explained. "I knowed he wouldn't, but I was fixed to scare him a little." He put the gun away and resumed his old position.

"Scare him a little, eh?" Sadar looked at Ben's deep-set, slate eyes. He studied the thick hands resting on the bar. They showed the hardness and color of skin that had been exposed to manual labor. "Why did Deedee start that beef?" Sadar asked.

Ben shrugged. "Partly because he don't like Reeves. Maybe because he didn't want him to find out something we're doing here."

What in the name of soup, mud, and potatoes could these old gees be doing that they had to conceal from Reeves? Sadar considered for a moment the sudden hunch that the feud might, somehow, be tied in with his own business in Sylvanite.

"You mine here in the old days?" he asked.

Ben shook his head slowly. "Very little underground work. Mostly I railroaded and blacksmithed." His eyes flicked across the room, came back to Sadar. "You know what, son?"

Sadar watched him quietly.

"If I was you, I wouldn't fool around Sylvanite much, unless it was just to go fishing," Ben said.

"Why?"

Ben wagged his head ponderously. There was calmness in the gesture, in his eyes, and finality in his refusal to say any more on the subject. Nor did he, although Sadar tried to elicit more information until he began to feel foolish. He fully realized, then, how Ben's impassiveness had got under Reeves's hide.

He gave up. "Where did Tarwater go?"

"Probably straight out the back door when the fight started. Sim won't even stay around a loud argument.

"Sensitive?" Sadar hadn't meant to sound sarcastic.

Ben's voice was harsh and his eyes glittered when he said: "He's got reasons. You ought to know part of them."

"I don't."

Ben grunted, staring like a basilisk.

Every blessed one of them thinks I know all about that calaverite was the thought running through Sadar's head, and he asked: "Where does Tarwater live?"

"On Tumbling River, around the north shoulder of the hill, about a mile and a half from here. I wouldn't go near there at night."

"Uh-huh?"

"Sim's hell for pets. One of them is a lion that hangs pretty close around the cabin."

"That how Tarwater got the crippled hand?"

Ben nodded. "Another pet lion . . . before you was born."

In spite of Ducray's taking him to the Fire Horse Club for some unknown reason, in spite of Ben's warning and his refusal to explain it, Sadar realized that neither man had seemed unfriendly. In fact, for a stranger, they had accepted him readily.

He laid a five-dollar note on the bar. "For the best steak I ever hope to eat."

Once in the cool night outside, he glanced back through the window. Ben was still motionless at the bar, staring at the wall.

He went down the silent street, past building after building, where the only inhabitant was decay. Sylvan Mountain was blue-black on his left. Glow from red and green neon in the remodeled, inhabited part of town made a garish aurora borealis on his right.

Between him and that glow was the silent past. He walked until an unused street brought him to the lower end of town. Here Tumbling River was loud and constant, oblivious of its own roar. The noises of its waters rumbled up from the deep cañon, rolled in waves against the dark shoulder of the mountain. I am here, the river seemed to say. For centuries I have poured and thundered from this rocky passage that I cut long before the first prospector set pick in Sylvan Mountain. What if ore trains, dynamite, the belch and stench of smelters and human hubbub overshadowed me for a fleeting instant? My sounds are eternal. I am here.

Cars making the curve that led to a long highway bridge flashed light on the tall, bareheaded figure standing high on a ledge about the rumbling stream. A jeepful of laughing youngsters shouted at him. The car hit the steel running plates of the bridge with a clatter. Girls squealed as the driver swung the vehicle from side to side.

Once the carload passed, there was something soothing, almost hypnotic in the ceaseless even sounds that came up from the cañon. The petty jarrings of the day were leveled into unimportance by the rumbling of water blended into night. Sadar stood motionless, trying to put together fragments from the day. He had the distinct impression that each person he had met—Ducray, Ralston, Tarwater, and Liggett—had been holding something back. Something that he was supposed to understand. And then there was Jackie Rouvière. Why, on both of their encounters, had he sensed that her carefree attitude was a front? Suddenly he yawned and realized that he was tired and sleepy.

Sadar started back to the hotel, passing three streetlights. Between him and the next one, he saw a small figure coming slowly along the walk. They met face to face, and the oncoming man stopped without a sound. It was Sim Tarwater. The light was at his back, and his eyes were in shadows, but Sadar felt the restlessness of those dark blue orbs as Tarwater faced him.

"You *are* Sam Rigdon's grandson?" Tarwater asked in his oddly soothing voice.

"I am."

"I knew it! So did Ben and Deedee. You might be Sam himself forty, fifty years ago."

Sadar wished the man would turn or shift his head. All he could see was a shadowy, thin face under the black dome of his undented hat.

"Is he still alive?" Tarwater asked.

Sadar nodded. "You knew him well?"

"I set great store by Sam." Tarwater's voice was as soothing as the river.

"Then you can tell me. . . ."

"Sam didn't know any more about it than I did. That's the truth, but there are people here, yet, who don't believe that. Remember that, young Sam."

The little man slipped past Sadar and went on down the street. His feet made no sound. He left the walk and angled toward the shadows of a vacant lot, and the night took him.

The everlasting sound of water came back strong and endless from the cañon.

You'll tell me more than that, Sim Tarwater, Sadar thought. *But I see you'll have to be handled gently.* He looked toward the darkness where Sim had disappeared. *Yes, Tarwater would be the man to talk to, and tomorrow wouldn't be too soon.*

Sadar cut over one street, working toward the oiled stretch that was the highway route through town. He felt that the evening had been well spent. He hadn't learned a thing, but Ben had warned him off, and, in a less direct manner, so had Tarwater. Ducray had sparred with him for information. Possibly all three men had a lead on the calaverite. Certainly Tarwater should have some good theories, having been a shifter at the Vivandière at the time of the robbery. So they knew who he was. Well, that couldn't be helped. All three men had been friendly, even though they had jumped at the right conclusion associated with his presence in Sylvanite.

Maybe they figured he had some first-hand information from his grandfather. Perhaps they wouldn't be so friendly when they discovered he didn't even know the details of the robbery and was trying to pry information from them. He thought of bitter, green-eyed Ralston, wondering again if Ralston had tried to get Rouvière's support in opening the Hibernian because Ralston thought the high grade was concealed there.

Well, let them all look for the twenty-seven sacks. His presence would serve to spur them to greater efforts. Let anybody who could find it, only the discovery had to be made public. That might prove to be the tricky part, unless he found the calaverite himself.

He stopped by a metal lamppost and looked at the black bulk of Sylvan Mountain. Somewhere in utter darkness in the honey-combed granite guts of the hill the high grade still must be. No doubt the mountain had been ransacked after the robbery, and probably prowled by hundreds in search of the stolen wealth in the years after the mines closed. He wondered why Deedee Ducray was so sure the calaverite hadn't been found in the years after the robbery? How he could be positive that it hadn't been brought to the surface the very night of the theft? Perversely he began to argue against the one fact he had to assume if his quest was to mean anything more than a futile gesture—the high grade was still in the mountain. Perhaps it had come out under loads of muck and had gone over the dump to be picked up by confederates.

He turned to go. The sound, emanating from a dark lane between two sagging buildings, was not loud. He heard it at almost the same instant something *clanged* against the fluted pillar of the lamp support. He caught a glimpse of a bright object in the light, then heard it strike a board fence somewhere across the street. For a breath he thought some mischievous boy had thrown a tin can. Then, from the darkness between the two buildings, he heard running sounds. He leaped from the sidewalk and ran toward the noise. The smooth wire of an old fence caught him hip-high and threw him on his side. He twisted for balance and grabbed the fence with one hand. The act broke his fall, but he sat down in damp weeds and a tangle of wire while staples screeched from unseen posts.

The running footsteps merged into the silence. From the cañon Tumbling River rumbled its muted, distant sound. He went back to the light, brushing at his pants. Under the lamp he paused to pluck the most troublesome of a hundred weed burrs from around his ankles. Then he went across the street and looked among the weeds by the fence where the missile had struck. At first he found nothing but burrs to replace the one he'd removed. Then he saw a faint metallic gleam where the weeds were highest, near the fence. He bent to retrieve the object, and for a moment, after he straightened, feeling the cold trimness of smooth metal, he thought he had the tip of a jointed casting rod. But when his fingers reached one end of the slender shaft, he knew for certain what he held. It was an arrow, approximately two feet long, made of tubular aluminum. The steel head was as deadly-looking as a trim, new automatic pistol.

Sadar glanced off into darkness, then knelt by the lamppost. Light caught on a bright nick made through the flaking paint, rust, and metal on the ridge of a flute. The arrow had been aimed stomach-high. He tried to remember exactly where he had been standing before he turned. As nearly as he could recall his position had been right at the post. He had swung away just as the archer released the deadly arrow. Whoever his assailant, he had not been trying to scare him or warn him off. The person who had stood in the shadows between those two buildings had aimed to drive that wedge of dark steel and the bright, slender tube clear through his guts.

Chapter Five

TREASURE HUNT

Golden sunlight lay heavy on Sylvan Mountain when Sadar came out of the Big Stope his second day in Sylvanite. He stood under the ring of burned-out carbide lamps, hanging from the wagon wheel, and looked at the pinkish-white dumps spotted in almost straight lines up the aspen-covered slopes.

That he had been warned off, that someone had tried to drive an arrow through his soft parts from the dark last night made him confident that the high grade was still around somewhere. He studied the slopes. Five hundred miles of workings up there. Still the ore must have been concentrated in a relatively small area, for, considering the number of dumps showing, five hundred miles of workings was not a great deal.

One day was gone. He had six left, six left to pinpoint, somehow, the exact spot where the high grade lay in the gloomy depths of those crumbling mines. Thirty years of neglect. That was a long time. Sadar had been in mines where the groaning movement of ground necessitated replacement of timbers every month. To make a stab at the mountain without a great number of facts, which he now lacked, would be folly, as futile as prodding with a stick at prairie dog holes in an effort to determine if there were a marble down one of the burrows.

He had decided he would first go to see Reeves. Housed at the remodeled brothel behind the hotel, Reeves recently had established new offices to direct the spending of Rouvière's money. When he had imparted that information to Sadar, Al Harris, the night desk clerk, had smiled hugely over the fact that Reeves either didn't know or had overlooked the original nature of his new offices.

Not wanting to waste any time, Sadar started around the corner. Last night he had paralyzed Reeves's legs with those two solid raps under the center joining of the ribs and had dumped him outside the Fire Horse Club with Jackie Rouvière and the others watching. Then, upon returning to the hotel a little more than an hour later, carrying the arrow that had almost cleaved his intestines, he had been given a polite note from Reeves, requesting an interview this morning. **I'm sure you will be interested** the last line had read. Sadar smiled thinly. He was interested, all right. Why, besides mayhem, would Reeves write a note like that only a short time after getting all the air and electricity knocked out of him?

Behind the Big Stope he passed the squares of a hideous formal garden where two men were working, and then saw across the street the mansion Harris had described. "It was a flourishing institution once," the clerk had said.

So far, the desk clerk had been a great help. He was intelligent, had a quiet sense of humor, and seemed to know what was going on about him. Besides, he seemed to dislike Reeves, an attitude that was beginning to attract Sadar to people who held it.

Last night, Harris hadn't been taken in entirely by Sadar's story about finding the arrow accidentally in the weeds, but he hadn't asked any questions. "It's a broad-head hunting arrow, one like Rouvière uses," he had said. "Last year he had a hunting party that used nothing but bows and arrows. Got three deer, they did."

Mrs. Mahogany, who seemed to have no profession other than appearing suddenly in any given conversation around the lobby, had crashed through center about them, scattering coherency as a large trout scatters minnows. She had a long story about a distant relative who could outshoot Robin Hood, but had allowed drinking to ruin his career. "Not unlike someone else we know," she had whispered. During pauses to check her air gauges, Sadar had managed to find out that Jack Ralston, then on good terms with Rouvière, had been a member of the archer's party the year before.

Now at the mansion, Sadar went up ten long steps to the porch, in three bounds. He cocked one eye at the repainted gingerbread around the outside edges of the porch, read a small, conservative sign that said—**Use This Door**—and went inside.

He came up short against a receptionist's desk, where sat the girl who had been handing lamps to Jackie Rouvière the night before. She recognized him and smiled. "Your beard! You shaved it off!"

"It got full of Lesser Aleutian Shovel-nose Dig-Digs," he said, and took in the room.

The receptionist paused before she realized he was joking, and then she giggled while Sadar noted two other girls working at typewriters. At the back of the room, behind a desk large enough to stow ten cases of .50 caliber ammunition, sat the long-jawed man who had been with Reeves in the Fire Horse Club last night. At a much smaller desk another man was talking to a well-dressed, middle-aged couple. Sadar heard him say: "Now, we have some very desirable old places that can be remodeled easily."

Sadar figured this outfit probably had slipped in quietly before the boom had started and grabbed up the best of the old houses.

The long-jawed man saw Sadar, got up, and crossed the room quickly. He held open a gate in the low partition. "Come right in, Mister Sadar. I'll see if Mister Reeves is busy."

"Thanks," Sadar said. He followed the man. Salmon Jaw was right. This guy could swim right along with male salmon and never be asked for credentials. Sadar waited at the huge desk while the secretary went through a high-paneled door. He listened shamelessly and attentively, but no sounds came through. Then Salmon Jaw came back, smiled, and waved him inside.

Reeves's dark oak desk was even more massive than the large one in the outer office. At his back a large bay window with Venetian blinds poured light on wallpaper with wide stripes of bilious blue and hang-over yellow. A tiny marble-faced fireplace, just right for burning old letters, nicked one end of the room. There was a shortage of chintz and mirrors, and the Venetian blinds were as prominent as an outhouse in the front yard, but on the whole, Sadar assessed, there might be some Victorian atmosphere in the joint—if one knew where to look for it.

Reeves waved at a red plush chair. "First off, I want to say I'm sorry about that little unpleasantness last night."

Sadar sat down. He saw no mark from his one head blow on the other's face. As he studied the unsavory face, he guessed that any mark was probably hidden under the clinched red whiskers. As he inspected the beard from across the desk, it looked as though Reeves had oiled the chin hair. *Holy mackerel,* Sadar thought as he restrained himself from feeling his own cheek bone, conscious that Reeves was looking at it.

"OK, it was all a sad mistake," Sadar said. He continued to study the other's face. Its expression was bland enough, but there lurked in the wide-set, reddish-brown eyes evidence that Reeves was offering the peace pipe for purposes of revenue only.

Rouvière's manager leaned back in his chair and clasped his hands behind his neck. "Our guests usually don't arrive the way you did yesterday. That caused me to look up your name. Simply curiosity, no more. After our little trouble, Pete Dill . . . that's my number one boy in the outer office . . . got you placed."

"That so?"

"You were first in the downhill at Little Cottonwood this spring. You took second in the jump at Steamboat before that . . . first on the Monarch Run . . . and twisted your knee just before the trials at Hillcrest. That right?"

Sadar nodded.

"Pete is a good man for names and facts." Visibly Reeves was pleased with himself. "That's why I hired him," he added, as if diverting too much credit.

"What's the pitch, Reeves?"

Reeves unclasped his hands and leaned forward. "I'd like to hire you for our ski instructor here next winter."

"That's a long time away."

"I mean now," Reeves said.

"Dry runs on soap chips?"

"I can find something for you to do till winter."

"Such as carrying in bags for hotel guests?"

"Hardly that!" Reeves shook his head impatiently. "After all, P.T.F."—he used the initials with elaborate carelessness—"leaves a great deal to my discretion." His eyes had settled on Sadar's bruised cheek bone. "I'm sure we can work together all right, no matter how badly we got started last night," Reeves assured Sadar, watching him keenly. "What do you think?"

I think you're a louse, and you could be the guy who cut loose an arrow at me last night, Sadar wanted to say. *You're working around to something under cover of that ski gag. If Salmon Jaw is such a whiz at names and facts, he probably already knew who I am.* Instead, Sadar stalled—"Well. . . ."—trying to guess how deep Reeves was playing. No doubt the man knew he was Sam Rigdon's grandson, and he probably felt confident he was after the calaverite. But did Reeves really know anything about the calaverite, or was he trying to angle in, believing that Sadar was trying to gather hard facts against what he was supposed to know?

Sadar decided to go along. "What's your deal?" he asked.

Reeves smiled with the air of a man who has set the hook solidly. "The first thing I have in mind is our vug treasure hunt. That's a little . . . ," he stopped, diverting his attention toward the door as it opened noiselessly. "Yes, Pete?"

Dill's long jaw moved up and down. "Jackie," he said.

Annoyance came instantly to Reeves's face. He recovered quickly and smiled. "Send her right in."

She was wearing jodhpurs, a fringed buckskin jacket, and a wide-brimmed black Mormon hat with a leather chin thong. Sadar's first impression was that it was a hell of a get-up, but, as he took a closer look, he observed the particular way she filled the garments and revised his opinion.

Jackie looked from one man to the other. "All areas of disagreement explored and conquered, I see."

Reeves laughed easily. "Yes, everything is ironed out. I'm hoping to hire Sadar as our ski instructor. In the meantime, I want to hold him here to make sure we have him next winter."

Jackie looked from face to face and said nothing. Sadar noted the change in her face. *A trace of fear,* he thought.

"Sadar's first job should be to hide the sack for the treasure hunt, don't you think, Jackie?" Reeves asked. "We can keep his hiring a secret, of course, so he won't be trailed by a mob the way I was last year." He turned to Sadar without waiting for an answer. "The vug hunt is a little attraction I started last year. We hide a sack of gold. On the last day of the celebration we print the clues, sort of like that radio identity program, you know. Of course, you can appreciate the terrific background of publicity we have ready-made."

"Sure," Sadar said, from the corner of his eye watching the serious way Jackie was studying both him and Reeves.

"How does it sound, Jackie?" Reeves asked.

"I couldn't think of a better man for the job," the girl said. "But that won't keep him busy till skiing season."

Sadar explored her face for sarcasm, tried vainly to recapture her tone and examine it for an insinuation.

"Oh, I'll find other things to do with him," Reeves said. "Those who work for me generally earn their money."

Sadar had an urge to walk out.

"I imagine," Jackie said. "Excuse me for having barged right in the middle of things. I just wanted to remind you not to forget that we're going riding today." She turned and went out as briskly as she'd entered.

Reeves appeared to be relieved.

"Last year you've no idea of the number of people who came swarming to hunt that treasure," he said. "Too many were undesirables, the camping-out class, you might say . . . so this year I've altered the procedure. Only those registered at the hotel, or living in one of our cabins, or those buying twenty-five dollars' worth of chips at the Poker Festival will be given the clues. I figure that will eliminate a large part of the non-spenders who come here just to hunt the treasure." He pursed his lips as if considering something distasteful. "Of course, we can't keep them away entirely."

Sadar squirmed in disgust.

"And, naturally, we can't hide gold," Reeves explained. "Just a sack with a chit redeemable for the amount."

Sadar nodded. The whole deal was as stagy as Reeves's efforts to cover his real motive in bringing Sadar to the office.

"You haven't given me an answer yet," Reeves said, having finished his sales pitch. "What do you say? Do you want to work with me?" He named a salary figure considerably out of line with the nature of the summer employment. "Of course, there may be other considerations later," he added significantly.

"What do you know about twenty-seven sacks of calaverite?" Sadar asked.

The abrupt question didn't startle Reeves. His expression was at once crafty and greedy. "Did I even mention anything about that?"

"No, but, just the same, what do you know about it?"

Reeves smiled. "Well, let's not get hasty. One thing at a time. You haven't answered my question about going to work."

Sadar considered several angles. Reeves didn't know anything about the high grade, perhaps, or maybe he knew plenty. It could be a ludicrous situation they were getting into, each playing the other for information that neither possessed. But time was short. Sadar had to work any angle that even looked like a bare chance.

"I'll take the job," he said.

"Fine!" Reeves shook two cigarettes from a pack on the desk, offering one to Rigdon.

They lit up and measured each other.

"Is it true that Jack Ralston went sour on Rouvière because Rouvière wouldn't help him open the Hibernian?" Sadar asked.

Reeves nodded. "The Hibernian is a poor bet."

"From what standpoint?"

"Mining. It was worked out years ago."

"You have any maps of the levels on the Vivandière?" Sadar asked next.

"All of them . . . here in the office." Reeves's eyes were steady.

"I'd like to see them."

"Later. After we work out certain agreements. How do I know you . . . ?"

The door to the outer office opened quietly, and Dill stepped in. "Mister Rouvière is at the real estate desk," he said quietly, holding the door closed behind him.

Reeves got up quickly. "All right, Pete." He turned to Sadar. "Well, I suppose you'll want to get started looking for a place to hide the sack." He went across the room and opened a door that led to the porch. "Let me know how things start to stack up. Take your time, look around. I imagine you'll want to familiarize yourself with . . . ah . . . landmarks and such. No hurry, you know."

"No hurry. I've got almost a week."

Sadar went out where the air was warm and clean. He stood on the porch several moments looking at Sylvan Mountain. Somewhere up there was the end of the old trail, a trail that Reeves, too, was trying to follow, without Rouvière's knowledge.

Across the street Jackie was watching the two men work in the formal gardens. In a graveled driveway sat a red jeep with a cub bear chained in the back seat. Sadar went across the street.

The cub whimpered, raked the air with its forepaws, and nuzzled Sadar's hand when he stepped up to the jeep. He turned the furry little brute around twice to unfoul the chain fastened to its collar, and scratched the animal's neck.

Jackie walked over. "You like Biff-Biff?"

"I took the job."

She laughed. "I mean the bear. We named him after Reeves."

Sadar grinned. "I'll bet Reeves appreciated that!"

"He actually did."

They looked at each other and laughed.

"So you're going to hide the sack for the treasure hunt. Rumor has it you're well-qualified by heredity for the job."

Sadar's face darkened. "Rumor is a damned liar!"

She looked at him keenly. "Sorry, I didn't realize how touchy you might be." She dropped her gaze. "Besides, you're not alone when it comes to bad associations with these mines. I wish . . . ," her voice trailed off.

"How come you know I'm Sam Rigdon's grandson?"

"Good Lord! With that beard you had. . . . I thought you were *trying* to look like your grandfather's picture with the fire laddies."

The old-timers had recognized him instantly; this girl had placed him from his likeness to the picture of his grandfather; and Pete Dill had used his memory of facts and names to come up with his identity. He couldn't have done any worse by arriving in a green fire truck and announcing his mission over a public address system.

"You didn't come into the office just to remind Reeves about that riding date," Sadar said.

"No. Frankly, I was curious about Biff's wanting to see you. After all, you know, he doesn't have any reason for liking you."

"Do you know why he wanted to see me?"

"I can guess his real reason. You didn't think Sam Rigdon's grandson was going to arrive in Sylvanite without people thinking he had a secret map to that vug kitty, did you?"

"If I did, I've shuffled the deck again." He studied her face. "Why should that old robbery suddenly get a lot of hot attention after all these years?"

"Maybe because Biff used it as capital in his treasure hunt publicity. Maybe because my father talked some of re-opening the Vivandière. But, mainly, because you're here."

"Did your father seriously consider opening the Vivandière to look for the calaverite?" Sadar asked.

She patted the cub, a wistful look crossing her face. "He considered it, but decided against it."

"And Ralston thinks it's in the Hibernian?"

She nodded. "I think he does. If it's still in the mountain, he may not be so silly as some people think. The two mines lie side by side for six thousand feet, and they were interconnected on almost every level. Perhaps Ralston knows something that nobody else does."

Jackie seemed to have made somewhat of a study of things in relation to that high grade, Sadar concluded. He disengaged Biff-Biff's sharp little teeth from his jacket sleeve, and unconsciously looked toward the mountain. This deal might become a little involved, what with everybody trying to get into the act. The high grade legally belonged to Rouvière, no matter where it was found, but, if anyone else besides Sadar or Rouvière himself found the cache, legality would probably get scant consideration, no more consideration than the hidden archer had shown last night.

"Al Harris tells me you kill deer around here with bows and arrows," Sadar said.

Jackie looked at him curiously. "What brought that up so abruptly?"

"It was just an idle thought."

"My father promoted a party last year. This year he's trying to get an area set aside for bow and arrow hunting only." She smiled. "I got one of the deer myself in that party last season."

"I thought it took a lot of power to bend one of those hunting bows."

"I'm no weakling, exactly. I was lucky, too."

"How'd Ralston do?"

"He wasn't much interested, except for taking the opportunity to talk mining to Dad. I think that's the only reason he went along."

"How about Reeves? Did he get a deer?"

"No, Mister D.A., Reeves didn't go. He just shoots a little on the range."

"Where'd Reeves go after our trouble last night?"

"He stopped at the Windlass Bucket. Business, you know. He owns the place."

Sadar playfully shoved the cub's head back as it leaned from the jeep to gnaw at the spare tire. "Did anyone ever tell you a bear belongs in the woods?"

"I'm finding that out. Last night he was busy tearing the upholstery out of my car while you and Biff were trying the same on each other."

Sadar grinned. "You seem to get along all right with the Fire Horse boys."

"That's right, I do."

He decided to plunge a little. "How come your father puts up with a man like Reeves?"

She gave him a cool look, becoming reserved instantly. "That is my father's business, Mister Sadar." She got into the jeep, started the motor, and tore down the driveway. Sadar ducked gravel as the vehicle toed in.

Sadar was thinking she was pretty touchy about her father, when he recalled how he had become a trifle hair-trigger at the subject of his grandfather.

Chapter Six

PAY DIRT

The office of the *Sylvanite Times*, two blocks down Main Street from the Big Stope, was not quite what Sadar had expected. Bright, blue-tinted windows looked out on Sylvan Mountain. The floor in front of a linoleum-topped counter was clean. He saw a modern-looking vertical press just forward of an ancient flatbed. Recalling Joe Tanner's moans about the expense of legal notices to clear title to land, Sadar guessed that the *Times* hadn't suffered from the property boom in Sylvanite.

The gray-haired man who greeted him across the counter was fat-jowled, clear-eyed, and looked like a fellow who knew his way around.

"Old files? Sure! Just treat 'em gently, will you?" He studied Sadar shrewdly. "Something in particular you want?"

"Yep! I'm looking for the story of the vug robbery here forty-five years ago."

The man's eyes played over Sadar's face keenly. "It's all in the files, son. Every word on it." He turned to shout to a blond lad who was squatting by a type case in the rear of the plant. "Show him where the old files are, Tommy! Better search him for a pocket knife and scissors, too!" he added with a grin.

Tommy sported an almost-new high school class ring and

a crew haircut. He measured Sadar's big frame with the candid appraisal of one young animal seeing outstanding physical qualities in another. "Those old papers are pretty dull," he warned.

And so they were, until Sadar gradually began to get the feel of those times that would not come again. At first the ads were the only lucid contents in pages of wandering, editorializing stories that attacked national politicians he had never heard of, or announced amazing strikes on every level of every mine on Sylvan Mountain. His interest began to pick up when he encountered his grandparents' names in social items.

He struck a million dollars' worth of pay dirt in a file that held the second half of a long-gone year. **Million Dollar Vug!!** a modest, one-column headline declared. He waded through the opinions of mining experts who explained that vugs were chambers left in solid formations by terrible gas pressures when the earth's crust was in a cooling state. Then he got to the specific million dollar vug on the fourth level of the Vivandière, eighteen hundred feet in, seven hundred and fifty feet below the surface, according to Superintendent Samuel T. Rigdon.

Who had made the statement that the incredibly rich calaverite lining the vug walls and lying on the floor was worth a million dollars was a matter between the editor and his conscience. Sadar read on, wading through conjecture, Latin proverbs, and synonyms of *astounding,* gleaning facts slowly amidst flowery flights.

The vug was rich. Sim Tarwater, night-shift boss on that level, "a gentleman not customarily given to overstatement or excessive verbiage of oral expression," admitted cautiously that he had "never seen the likes before." It was on Sim's shift that a Sullivan operator and his chuck tender, driving a cross-cut toward the Hibernian sideline, and "little dreaming of the remarkable discovery they were on the verge of consummating," became puzzled when a three-foot length of steel rattled through "into thin and empty space." They decided they had broken into an old slope of the Hibernian, and the driller sent his helper for Sim Tarwater, who ordered a hole shot lightly. He went back into sickening powder smoke soon afterward and discovered the shot had broken an opening into a small chamber where calaverite lay "as jewels in the strong room of an Oriental potentate." Sim stood guard and sent the driller to wake Sam Rigdon. Rigdon looked, swore, and sent Sim Tarwater to rouse Marcus Besse, owner of the Vivandière and P.T.F. Rouvière's uncle. Besse looked, scooped, and lapsed into French for ten minutes.

While the astounded drilling crew under Mr. Tarwater's direction enlarged the vug opening, a brand new vault door, then in the freight yards, was diverted from its destination at the new courthouse, whisked up the mountain, and before the first tiny flush of dawn had touched the sylvan green of the slopes, this formidable barrier of the finest modern steel was concreted in place at the vug entrance.

In the next issue the paper increased its estimate of the vug treasure by two hundred thousand dollars and took a tolerant attitude toward the fact that everyone, in the haste attendant upon placing the vault door, had forgotten to inquire what, if any, was the combination to the lock. Several telegrams to St. Louis settled that matter. In no time at all Marcus Besse was making a show place of the vug.

As he scanned the brittle pages, Sadar walked with Besse and Sam Rigdon along the main drift of Vivandière Number

Four, entered a cross-cut where Sim Tarwater and another trusted employee put in twelve-hour shifts to see that no unauthorized persons got near the vault door, waited while either Besse or Rigdon opened the steel barrier, and stared at natural wealth in one of nature's richest storerooms.

He was an invisible, detached spectator in the vug while hundreds came to look. Marcus Besse was in his glory. To many, especially the ladies, the Frenchman gave pieces of calaverite as souvenirs. He had a high-backed horsehair chair installed for the use of delicate visitors suddenly overcome from the sight of so much wealth. Sometimes, when visitors were few, he sat in it himself, staring for long periods at the high grade.

Not everyone was allowed to see the treasure, especially persons such as a notorious brothel character who was stopped in the dry-room and divested of, not one, but three high grader's belts before being sent on his way. Still, either Rigdon or Besse escorted magnates, madams, and visiting bigwigs past faithful Sim Tarwater. A touring English nobleman almost lost composure at sight of the calaverite. "Amazing!" he had said. "Really amazing!"

A learned geologist inquired nervously of the probability of cave-ins. He shivered in the cold, sat down in the horsehair throne, and began an abstruse lecture on the cleavage of tellurium ores. A reigning madam, her finery hidden under a stiff slicker, listened only briefly. "That may be true, professor," she had allowed, "but my business will outlast this little pile of shiny rock."

For ten days the vug was a show room. Then Besse announced a date when the calaverite would be taken to the surface. Gamblers ran pools on the amount of final settlement. A literary society ran a sweepstakes to raise funds to bring an opera singer to Sylvanite. Mrs. Samuel T. Rigdon had approved the project as "most worthwhile."

On the day set for the removal of the treasure, that had been sacked the night before, Besse, Rigdon, and Tarwater went to the vug with five selected miners, all relatives of Besse. Guards were thick at the Number Four portal. Sight-seers were swarming around the mine as close as they were allowed to come. A drunk fell into an old prospect hole and broke his leg. The crews of two light engines, supposed to be on their way to the Evening Star mine, delayed their trip for two hours to watch the removal of the high grade, while the superintendent of the Evening Star, all cars on his siding filled and his bins overflowing, swore he'd sue hell out of the railroad.

Besse's plan was to take the calaverite to the main drift of Number Four, down a raise to Number Five level, and bring it to sunlight at the Five portal. Guards were not so much in evidence there, but just as numerous as around the upper level. The owner's choosing of this round-about route was a precaution brought about by the rumor that an unusually bold gang of hold-ups were planning to create a diversion by blowing up a large store of flour on the hillside. Under cover of the cloud of milled wheat the thieves were going to seize the calaverite and escape on fast horses to a mountain hide-out.

The story was a credit to somebody's imagination, although some credence could be taken from the fact that two boxes of dynamite and four sacks of flour had been found near the Number Four portal. Sam Rigdon pointed out that the powder had been cached, undoubtedly, by some teamster on a freight haul to mines farther up the mountain, it being a common practice of muleskinners to steal at least two boxes from every load of dynamite they hauled, for sale to prospec-tors at reduced rates.

The flour, Rigdon said, had been there for some time, so long that dampness had spoiled it and run the printing on the sacks. It had been stolen, investigation tended to show, from the wagon of a teamster hauling supplies to a boarding house at the Glory Me tunnel. The muleskinner had left his team unattended one day to stagger off to a nearby spring. The unfamiliar liquid had left him somewhat indisposed for ten or fifteen minutes, and someone had taken advantage of his sad condition to loot the wagon of the flour, caching it for recovery later. Rain that day had ruined it, so the unknown party or parties had not bothered to recover the wheat. So Sam Rigdon theorized.

Besse may not have believed the fantastic story of the plot, but he was cautious and wanted to take no chances. Eighteen hundred feet in, seven hundred and fifty feet down, behind steel, with men on guard, the calaverite had been safe enough. Bringing it to daylight was something else. Sacks of country rock were to be taken from the Number Four portal as a ruse, while the real wealth was being lowered to Five level, for less conspicuous removal.

The plan was sensible and a credit to Besse's Auvergne ancestry. Just one hitch developed. When Besse and his party entered the vug, the twenty-seven sacks were gone. The thieves had left nothing but the high-backed chair. From the vug a small opening led to an abandoned stope in the Hibernian, just ten feet away. Besse went wild. He invoked curses on the thieves; on the owner of the Hibernian, Theodore Ralston; on high graders in general and their ancestors; on Sam Rigdon for not knowing exactly how close to that old stope the vug had been; and on himself for leaving the calaverite underground any longer than it would have taken to sack it and get it to safety.

Those charged with taking the fake ore went about their

business on schedule, not knowing the vug had been looted. The crowd outside saw the sacks hustled into spring wagons and whisked away under heavy guard. They were satisfied. Having counted twenty-seven sacks, observing, too, that their weights seemed considerably above average for calaverite, sightseers increased their estimate of the treasure's value by varying amounts.

The spring wagons raised a dust cloud as they went toward the Sylvanite State Bank. Sightseers drifted away. The two engine crews made their belated run up to the Evening Star and cursed the superintendent as heartily as he had damned them. Everything returned to normal.

Except inside the vug, where Marcus Besse sat on his horsehair chair, his tears bright in the candlelight. Then he rose and began to curse again.

Two days later Pinkerton men mingled with miners in bars and brothels. Some were employed at the Vivandière, on Level Four; two were working at the Hibernian, with Theodore Ralston's approval, Besse having decided, when he cooled down, that Ralston had nothing to do with the robbery, but that some of his outlaw miners certainly had. If the detectives found out anything definite, no public announcement was ever made.

Two theories sprang up. One held that the sacks had been taken by Hibernian miners who had been smart enough to realize how close the vug lay to that abandoned stope. After the vug was first uncovered, there had been plenty of time to run a narrow ten-foot drift to tap it. The other theory contended that the passage had been made by Vivandière miners from the vug *to* the stope, with the full knowledge of Sam Rigdon and Sim Tarwater—Rigdon being the only man besides Besse who had known the combination to the vault lock. These theorists held that the drift was a blind to throw suspicion on the

Hibernian, and that the passage had been made on three successive night shifts by Vivandière miners, who cleverly had sealed their work with rock and talc after each operation.

Those who had never been underground agreed, unaware that even a half-baked miner would have detected something amiss in the appearance of the wall. But even smarter men admitted cautiously that there could be something to the story—after they learned that Besse's high-backed chair had always sat against the end of the vug where the tiny drift opened.

Still others, confusing cause and effect with the sure fumbling of stupidity, declared that Besse had stolen the high grade from himself. This, Besse raged, was the unkindest cut of all. Any man who would try to fool innocent bystanders with country rock in sacks would do anything, his detractors shouted.

On the whole, everyone conceded that the calaverite was gone.

Veteran miners could not agree when they tried to determine from which direction the tunnel had been run. All drill holes had been picked out carefully, or else the loose nature of the gangue material had sloughed to leave no marks. Water in the old stope reached a four-foot depth in the upper end, where the walls had caved to form a block; running almost to the stope end of the little drift, that pool had received muck from the passage, if the tunnel had been made *from* the stope to the vug. Whether the muck under that water was fresh or not was hard to say, especially after miners, attempting to drain the pool away, brought down fresh material from the stope walls by accident.

If the drift had been made *from* the vug to the stope, the resulting muck could have been carried past conniving Tarwater, sack by sack. A good many hard-headed people pointed out that it would have been just as easy to carry the calaverite out the same way, without going to all the trouble of running an opening to the stope in order to divert suspicion.

Short-handled tools left in the stope proved nothing, although the detectives pawed over them and scowled thoughtfully.

Sim Tarwater said he had heard light shots that seemed to come from the direction of the vug when he was on night guard duty in the cross-cut just off the main drift, and that he had reported them to Sam Rigdon. Besse admitted that Rigdon had mentioned Sim's uneasiness over the sounds, but that he himself had dismissed them as coming from other parts of the Vivandière, since Tarwater said they coincided with the usual blasting time in the Vivandière.

The last shots that Tarwater had heard, he recalled as having come two or three hours before the graveyard shift began—*the evening before the robbery was discovered*. Assuming that those last shots marked the time the thieves actually reached the vug, Besse pointed out that the culprits couldn't have had time to carry the sacks out of the Hibernian. To do so they would have been forced to travel by difficult, little-used routes to avoid detection in the mine, and then they would have had to face a high grade checking system at any portal they tried on the Hibernian. The same high grade checks prevailed on every level of the Vivandière, assuming that the thieves had gone from the Hibernian *back into* the Vivandière using any one of the numerous interconnecting cross-cuts, he was careful to add.

Mines on either side of the Hibernian and Vivandière were also connected by workings, and some of those mines didn't have rigid checking systems at the portals. But Besse pointed out a hard fact to get around: twenty-seven sacks of ore was a lot of weight to carry up raises and through old stopes to reach the surface at some distant point, always assuming that there had been only two or three hours' time to do so. Time-keepers' records at every portal at both mines showed that not one miner had been late coming off the shift.

The writer introduced his own theory. Tarwater, he said, could have been mistaken about the shots. The thieves might have had a whole shift to move the sacks, and might have carried their loot out through an opening a long way from either mine. It was possible for a miner who knew the honey-combed mountain well to have gone mile on mile underground. A Cousin Jack veteran proved that. He entered the Dolly shaft, one half mile from Sylvanite, and six hours later emerged at the Digman mine three miles away. His act proved something, but not where the calaverite was.

Before the robbery dwindled to nothing in the newspapers, Besse offered a ten thousand dollar reward for information leading to the conviction of the thieves and the same amount for information leading to the recovery of the sacks. He repeated that he was convinced the high grade was still underground, and added that, "as president of the Mine Operators' Association, I have the backing to say that from now on very stringent checks will prevail."

Ten weeks after the robbery Marcus Besse announced the resignations of Samuel T. Rigdon and Sim Tarwater.

Mr. Besse wishes to state emphatically that no shadow of culpability attaches to the two employees, that they leave of their own volition. Mr. Besse personally minimizes the degree of negligence involved. . . .

Two weeks later Rigdon Sadar's mother was born and his grandmother was dead.

He closed the file and put it back on the shelf where other dead years rested quietly. He came back to the present slowly, as a man waking to unfamiliar surroundings. The blond printer was sorting material from a wrecked form. A small gray-headed woman had joined the staff and was typing fast and rhythmically at a desk near the front. At the counter, the owner was talking to a farmer who wanted a sign that said **No Hunting and Fishing**.

Sadar looked up the mountain through the window. Waste piles, blotched against the green, looked weathered and hard. Old mine buildings seemed to slump and show their age. The spell he'd built while reading had been binding and vivid. But this was today. He walked toward the door.

"Find out what you wanted?" the editor asked.

Sadar nodded. "Thanks."

The editor laughed. "You did better than old Besse, then!"

Sadar stood outside, staring at Sylvan Mountain. *No culpability. So Besse minimized the degree of negligence. Negligence!* He scowled at the line of dumps. The old Army game. Someone had to take the rap. So Sim Tarwater ended up with a haunted, restless look, and, from his grandfather, Sadar had inherited all the gnawing unfairness of a lie. He could fully understand the reasons for his grandfather's savage burst of temper when the subject of the robbery had first come up. And now he knew why the old man had never cared to talk about it. It was more important than ever that he find the calaverite. And the task looked much harder.

He went over his experiences since coming to Sylvanite. The person who had loosed the arrow, no doubt, was the person who knew most about the high grade. Deedee Ducray? Ducray had been in bed with a crippled hip. Anyway, the thought of that brown-eyed old man skulking in the dark with a bow didn't fit. Ben didn't fit, either. Besides, he'd warned Sadar. Why should he follow up that warning by trying to kill him soon afterward? Ralston was bitter and hard and had a violent temper, but Ralston was interested in the Hibernian. He owned it, and could control any efforts, beyond useless prowling, to search the Hibernian for the calaverite. Besides, he hadn't even known who Sadar was, not last night, at least.

Jackie could bend a mean bow, but she was a woman. He realized this thinking was illogical and beside the point. He couldn't see her trying to kill him. And P.T.F. Rouvière wasn't the kind who had to skulk around in the dark, even if he had wanted Sadar killed. Sim Tarwater? No, Sim hadn't had his bow and arrows when Sadar had encountered him before the aluminum tube came whispering from the dark to clang against the lamppost. To give the devil his due credit, Sadar didn't think even Reeves, as much of a crooked bastard as the red-bearded man might be, was the kind who would resort to a sneak trick to kill someone. Reeves's methods would be to chisel in, just as he had tried to do in his underhanded conversation this morning.

Sadar frowned. Standing there in the bright sunlight, he couldn't readily believe that any of the people he'd met in Sylvanite would try to kill him. And yet someone had.

He went back and had another look at the bright nick on the lamppost. He crossed the fence that had tripped him and looked at the weeds between the two buildings where the archer had stood. Broken stalks and wilting leaves provided no more than he already knew. There was more evidence of the person's flight among the rank weeds in the alley.

Sadar left the scene not even mildly disappointed. He hadn't expected to find anything. Nonetheless, impatience was growing in him, a nervous urge for action. He wanted to start prowling the mountain and the old mines, even though, as he forced himself to acknowledge, such a course would be the least productive he could follow. No, the way to find those twenty-seven sacks was not to begin aimless exploring of five hundred miles of abandoned workings. At least not until he had exhausted his chances of learning as much as he could in Sylvanite. But time was passing.

Old Charley had just finished servicing a car as Sadar approached. The old man wiped his hands on a rag of striped blue ticking, then jammed it in his hip pocket, and went unerringly toward his broken-springed throne. His squint at Sadar was exactly the same as when he'd first seen him the night before.

Sadar grinned. "I came back to talk some more about Delmonico's menus."

"By gum! The Alaska boy! I knowed you . . . and yet I didn't! No beard makes a big difference. Funny thing about hair. . . ." He dived into a story about a bald-headed bartender in Tincup, who, at sixty-five, had grown a mane of jet-black hair. "He saved the leavin's in whisky glasses and rubbed 'em on his head three, four times a day."

"I didn't know anybody in those days ever left any whisky in a glass."

Charley cackled. "They left plenty of *that* fellow's liquor!" He studied Sadar for several moments. "I shoulda knowed you was Sam Rigdon's boy . . . grandson."

Sadar realized the news of his identity was traveling fast enough.

Charley winked confidentially. "Guess you know what folks are saying?"

"I can guess. Well, they're right. I'm digging up the loot tonight."

Charley laughed. "That's pretty good!" He squinted and

leaned forward. "Never was no robbery, you know."

"No?"

"Mark my words, young Sam . . ."—his fist went up and down on a spring—"that ore went to the smelter right enough . . . only it ran so damn' low that old Besse was ashamed of all the show he'd made of things, so he just faked the robbery to cover up being a jackass." Charley let his last dozen words out rapidly.

"Why did my grandfather quit, if that's true?"

"He got sore at Besse and wanted to tell the truth. So Besse just up and fired him. Then he fired Sim because he stuck up for Sam."

Sadar started up the street toward the Windlass Bucket, then stopped to say: "You might be right, Charley."

"I am right!" Charley's hip pocket had become entangled in a broken spring, and he began to curse. "Dang' seat! It ought to be fixed sometime!"

Chapter Seven

A LITTLE HIGH GRADE HELL

The Windlass Bucket was crowded. Bright shirts, big hats, a few imitation prospectors in boots and derbies. A good many sober citizens were trying to catch a quick meal or a quick drink. At one end of the bar a woman with an upswept hairdo and a rusty-looking silk gown with an enormous bustle was wailing: "She's only a birr-rd in a gilded cage! Just a birr-rd in a gi-hill-ded ca-hage!"

Sadar felt the same way until he spied Ralston sitting at a deuce table against the wall. He walked over, pulled out the second chair, and sat down. "Hope you don't mind, Ralston." Sadar looked around the room and grinned. "Sort of noisy . . . but it's colorful in a way."

"It stinks," Ralston said. He studied Sadar for several moments. "Been up the hill?"

"Yep! I went up to see if the calaverite was where my grandpop said. It was . . . so tonight I'm going south with it."

Ralston's sneer came readily. It was on the surface, anyway, and merely had to deepen a little. "Let me know what time, and I'll furnish you with a free truck."

Sadar grinned. "It's a deal." He studied Ralston a moment, deciding that there was something deeply defensive in the man. "Your boy Charley tells me old Marcus Besse never really was robbed."

"Charley has his interpretation of everything, including a theory that changing oil in a motor is a waste of money." Ralston grimaced in disgust as the singer began her version of "Frankie and Johnny." "That vug was tapped, never fear. But the stuff went through some crooked assay office a long, long time ago, and what *they* didn't knock down soon went for women and whisky before you and I were born. The gold is buried, all right . . . at Fort Knox."

"I suppose so," Sadar said, and then offered to buy Ralston a beer.

Their drink and food orders were given to a harried waitress, who kept looking back over her shoulder as if she had forgotten something.

"You own the Hibernian by yourself?" Sadar asked.

Ralston nodded.

"What will you take for it?"

Ralston reacted much harder than Sadar had expected. His eyelids shot up, and his lips half parted. Then his jaw hardened, and his green eyes grew luminescent with anger. "It's not for sale at any price!"

Sadar shrugged.

Ralston's voice started to rise. "Did Rouvière send you to buy it for him?"

"No."

"You were in Reeves's office this morning. By God! He's cooking up a deal. Why, that dirty. . . ."

"Take it easy," Sadar said. "I was asking for myself."

Ralston's temper subsided, but he continued to study Sadar angrily.

The singer tossed back a straight shot, cleared her throat, and began a rollicking song of "The days of old, the days of gold. . . ."

The food arrived. They ate in silence, Ralston giving sullen attention to his plate. Sadar's several attempts to strike up a conversation went unnoticed.

After lunch they parted in silence at the cashier's register, Ralston giving Sadar a last glance, a composite of malevolence leavened with a big dab of suspicion. As Sadar took a step to the door, the garage man started to say something, then, apparently changing his mind, walked out abruptly.

At the Fire Horse Club, Sadar heard the poker game going on in the casino and found Ben Liggett sitting at the long table in the barroom, reading a copy of the *Sylvanite Times*. Sadar noted that in daylight Ben's brown face seemed less solemn, his dark eyes more expressive. However, his voice was no less sepulchral as he thrust the paper toward Sadar. "Guess you never seen this."

Sadar took the paper and sat down. The copy was a few days less than a year old, and the entire front page was devoted to the very matter he had spent three hours looking up in old files that morning. Sam Rigdon and Marcus Besse were shown in two dark pictures. The whole east face of Sylvan Mountain was there in a still darker picture, under the banner-style question: **Does A Stolen Fortune Still Lie Here?**

Sadar's eyes skimmed through the columns. The story was substantially the same as he had dug from the files, although shot full of glamour and romance. The whole page was a clever publicity build-up for Reeves's treasure hunt. He tossed the paper on the table, wondering why Ben had gone to all the trouble to dig up the copy.

"It doesn't say very much about Sim Tarwater," Sadar said.

Ben nodded slowly. "Reeves himself went up to see Sim to get a big yarn. I happened to be there. Sim warned Reeves that, if there was one dirty crack about him, Reeves and the newspaper wouldn't be there the day after it come out. It was the first time in about forty-five years I ever heard Sim say a harsh word. It was enough to chill the red-hot blood in you, believe me!"

Sadar's mind went back to little Sim's dark hatchet face with the strangely uneasy eyes. "What's the story about Sim . . . after the robbery?"

Ben rested the calf of one leg on the corner of the table. Dried mud was caked on his shoe, Sadar saw. Fine, dry drilling mud.

"The vug business is what touched things off. Sim was pretty bitter about being canned, of course, and no mine would hire him. The owners clamped down so hard on high-grading that no one could make a decent living at it." Ben didn't smile when Sadar grinned. "One night at exactly three o'clock the owners had fourteen crooked assay offices blowed sky-high. Looking at it now, I can see the owners had plenty on their side. Them offices handled most of the high grade swiped . . . some of 'em was baby smelters. They could run a quarter ton of stuff in twenty-four hours. Did it, too."

Far more vividly than the yellowed files, the glint in Ben's slate eyes and the thick vibrancy of his voice took Sadar back forty-five years.

"You see, Sim's brother lived next to one of them offices, and a piece of furnace come down through the roof and killed him in bed. That made Sim pretty near a madman. The miners were sore about the assay offices and a few other things the owners done. They put in California rounds . . . they figured out ways to beat the high-grade checks. One thing led to another. Sim was right in the middle of all the trouble. The owners brought in thugs when the governor wouldn't send the militia in." Pausing, Ben stretched his other leg atop the first and stared at the panorama of

Sylvanite. "The miners went out. The owners brought in more toughs and thugs. In all, eleven miners got killed in the trouble that came after that. Five of 'em was from the Hibernian. Like everybody else I always figured those five were men the detectives had identified as having robbed the vug, and that the owners took and used the cover of the trouble to have 'em fixed."

Ben's voice was large in the long room. "Then the miners put two boxes of dynamite under a barracks where the toughs lived. Some say Sim planted both of 'em, but it wasn't him. But he was on the other end of one of the battery boxes when the time come to let 'er go. There was two leads from the powder. One of 'em . . . the one that went to Sim's detonator . . . got busted in the dark. He jammed the plunger just as the second man pushed his. The barracks went up, and nineteen toughs went to hell. There was fifty or more in the hospital and eight or nine of them died, too."

Ben studied his hands for several moments. Sounds of the poker game came clearly from the casino.

"Sim went a little simple," Ben continued. "He never would believe his lead was busted that night and didn't go off. Still don't, as near as I can figure. He swore he'd blowed those men up . . . not that he didn't intend to right enough . . . but, after he saw parts of bodies with boards clean through 'em and heard the groaning and screaming, he almost lost his senses. He wanted to give himself up, but the miners wouldn't let him do that. They hid him for a week up on Lost Man Creek before he began to come around. I guess he finally saw the damage was done and couldn't be helped. He went up and built that cabin above the big falls on Tumbling River and began to think more of animals than men. Sim never set foot in a mine, after that. It's only in the last few years that he's even started coming to town any more than he had to."

Silence held in the long room, until Sadar asked: "Nobody ever got caught? The story never got around . . . about Sim?"

"It got hinted at, sure. But there never was any proof. Besides Sim, there's only three other men in Sylvanite who know what I've just told you."

"You and Deedee Ducray, and. . . . ?"

"You."

Sadar stared.

Ben's wide face was unreadable. He rose and went behind the bar, returning with a bottle and two glasses.

"You're the third man. Being Sam Rigdon's grandson, you'll probably keep your mouth shut. You wondered about Sim last night. I figured you'll be going up to see him, and I wanted you to know about him before you got to prodding him too hard." He poured two drinks and took his at a gulp. "Some things don't rest so heavy when you talk about 'em. I fought Marcus Besse and the rest as hard as anyone. Now I'm back fighting his nephew, and it seems like a damn' senseless thing for men getting as old as some of us are. I'm a little bit tired." He shook the bottle. It was almost empty. "But I guess it's the thing to do."

"You think the vug robbery touched off all the trouble?" Sadar asked.

"I know it did. It was several months in coming, but that's what started it, and that's why Sim don't like to talk about any part of it."

"You think the thieves were killed and the calaverite is still in the hill?"

Ben offered another drink. Sadar shook his head, and Ben tipped the bottle and drained it.

"Sure the stuff is still underground! And there it can stay. Sim Tarwater may know, or have some idea where it is, even if we all know he didn't have anything to do with the stealing.

Sim could make a good guess, maybe, because he knew that hill like no one else did, but Sim won't talk." Ben turned the empty bottle slowly in his big, brown-mottled hands. "Maybe Sam Rigdon made a good guess. . . ."

Sadar rose. "If he did, he never mentioned it to me."

Ben nodded, his slate eyes searching Sadar's face. "I didn't suppose he ever did." He set the bottle on the table and stood up.

"One more thing, Ben. What can you tell me about Jackie Rouvière?"

"Only one local story a day, young Sam," he replied. "Now, if you'll wait a minute."

When Ben came back from behind the bar, he offered Sadar a Frontier Model Colt. For the life of him, Sadar couldn't read a thing in Ben's eyes or expression. "Why?" he asked.

"I know you won't quit. I knowed it last night when I told you to." He put the gun on the table and pushed it toward Sadar. "Have you got one of your own?"

Sadar shook his head. "What were you warning me about last night?"

"I ain't sure. If I had been, I'd come right out and say so."

"You're sure enough to offer me your gun," Sadar said.

"It never hurts to play safe." Ben's eyes were hard and steady. "You going to take it?"

"With a handgun I couldn't hit the side of a barn in daylight . . . let alone someone after dark." Whether or not the last part of the sentence meant anything to Ben was impossible to tell.

"Well,"—Ben sighed heavily—"I suppose you want to know now where you can find Deedee and Sim. . . ."

Dressed in digging clothes, Ducray was sitting on a half

sack of blacksmith's coal near a wire gate in front of a small, weather-beaten house surrounded by vegetable gardens.

He stood up and grinned as Sadar neared. Eyeing the tall, unstooped figure, his big hands hanging idly at his sides, Sadar wondered just what might have happened if Ducray's hip hadn't gone bad when he was forcing action on Reeves. Still, an old man was old . . . and age was an insurmountable handicap against a powerful young man like Reeves.

"How's the hip?" Sadar asked.

"Good enough. It gets all right in between being hurt. What with the mine and the garden and one thing and another, I ain't got time to pamper it." He sat back down on the sack.

"You mean you're only carrying one sack up the hill?" Sadar asked, grinning.

"I could do it, don't you worry, but Jackie Rouvière saw me one day on the trail when my hip had gone bad . . . and now she makes me take one of the hotel's horses. I'm waiting for her now." Ducray grinned. Evidently Jackie hadn't found much opposition in forcing her help on him.

Sadar wondered if Reeves had ever attempted to lecture Jackie on the evils of extending help and courtesy to his enemies.

"Why didn't you say something last night, when you recognized me?" Sadar asked.

Ducray chuckled. "Why didn't you say who you were . . . instead of using that bum gag about fluorspar? I was right on the point of asking if you was any relation to Sam Rigdon, and then you popped up with that business about spar. Anybody knows there ain't a hundred pounds of it on this side of the range."

"All right, it was a poor stall." Sadar smiled. "Want to go up the hill with me and help carry the calaverite back?"

"Next year, young Sam . . . after you get things mucked out and all your timbering done."

Sadar laughed. "Ben says she's still there."

"Ben's dead right, too." Ducray rose again. "But let me show you something." He pointed along the base of the mountain where rails lay almost buried in dump wash. A blue truck was backing slowly toward a great, sloping depression edged by trash. "See that hole? When I was a kid, an old stope come in there. The mines close to it dumped cinders in it for years . . . the city has used it for a garbage dump ever since it caved in, but it's still quite a hole. That was just one of the littler stopes in this district. I remember others so big you couldn't see the candle of a man standing on the other side."

"The guy on the other side should have lit *his* candle," Sadar replied.

"He . . . what?" Ducray grinned. "You're like Sam, all right." He looked up the mountain. "There's diggings in that hill that got enough timber in 'em to build a good-sized town. Once a switch engine on the Evening Star grade busted into a square-setted stope that run to grassroots. People who saw that engine said it didn't look no bigger down there than a grasshopper in a dry-goods case." Ducray nodded seriously. "That just gives you an idea of what the hill is like inside. Sure, I think the calaverite is there, too . . . but there may be a million tons of muck and a hundred feet of water on top of it."

"You think, then, that the thieves didn't have time to get the sacks to the surface?"

Ducray sat down on the sack again and plucked a dried clout of drilling mud from the frayed cuff of his overalls.

"Yep! That's one time I agreed with Marcus Besse."

"Do you think they got killed in the trouble after the robbery?"

Ducray nodded. "Four or five of the men who got killed

were miners that were working mighty close to that old stope in the Hibernian. They were the ones who would have had the best show to run the drift to the vug. The owners couldn't prove a thing on 'em, so, when they had a good chance, they had those four, five men shot up by toughs."

"Does Sim Tarwater figure the same way you do about the robbery?" Sadar asked.

"Sim doesn't ever talk about it. If you go real easy, you might get him to talk some to you, since Sim thought mighty well of your granddad." Ducray looked up with frank appeal in his eyes. "Don't push Sim too hard. He's lived in hell up until a few years ago, but, if you do get him to talking, which would be more than anybody else has for the last forty-five years, you'd better listen close, because Sim sometimes gets his mind so far ahead of his words they don't make sense."

"I'm going to try him," Sadar said. "Well, I'd like to stick around and talk to your girlfriend, but I won't find calaverite that way."

"Save me a sack or two," Ducray said as Sadar started away. He heard the beginning of yet another sentence as he slipped out of earshot. "Ain't my girlfriend, so if'n you got a mind. . . ."

Chapter Eight

OLD MAN OF THE MOUNTAIN

Beyond the weed-grown lots where human predators had nibbled away most of the deserted shacks for firewood and stray boards, Sadar came to the toe of the mountain. Huge dumps with deteriorating ore bins that opened over rusting rails lay as far as he could see along the base of the slope.

He climbed to the tunnel level of the first dump he reached. Flaking paint on the dry-room read: **Hibernian Mines, No. 6.** Rusting locks showed on every door, although missing boards had left openings where twenty men could have sifted rapidly into the building. On the portal a heavy door with a broken top hinge was jammed in half-open position, a rust-encrusted chain and lock dangling from it. Water was running from under it. From rotting sills beside the track, he saw, there had been at one time a shed from the portal to the main building. The typewritten notice on the door was fresh enough. **Trespassers will be prosecuted!** It was signed: **John R. Ralston.**

He went back to the edge of the dump and looked up the mountain, seeing an even break in the treetops, a line that marked the railroad grade that Ben had said would lead to a trail that went around the shoulder of the mountain to Tarwater's cabin on Tumbling River.

Sadar went straight up the slope. Growth was lush. At times, dense aspens completely hid the town below him. Ferns, willows, and rank plants with gourd-like leaves dragged against his legs. For stretches he might have been on a hillside ungutted of its gold, untouched on the surface. But here and there he stumbled over rusted cable, remnants of carbide cans, rotting ties with spikes still driven. He crossed old wagon roads where quick-growing aspens were rotted in unrutted surfacing.

He stopped on the fifth level of the Hibernian. Clear water was running in a large stream between heavy rocks that completely blocked the portal.

For a moment, as he stood looking at the town from the dump where corroding rails extended into the air above rotting posts from which the ties had long since fallen to go back to earth in the trees below, he imagined Sylvanite to be alive and roaring once more. His mind's eye saw throngs of miners tramping the streets, wagons raising dust, smoke slanting over the green valley from huge smelters at the edge of town, mansions and big carriage houses sitting proudly, unweathered, and the scarred mountain around him teeming like an anthill.

Then he turned and was brought back to reality as he saw the cave portal where ferns were growing next to upthrust lagging in the black overburden that capped the cave-in. The ski course—more reality—lay between him and the next line of dumps running up the mountain. They had to be the Vivandière levels, since the two mines lay side by side for six thousand feet. Five hundred miles of gloom and desolation. Ponderous slabs falling for thirty years, longer in older parts of the workings. Sylvan Mountain had had a long time to grind inward as it tried to seal internal scars. This one caved portal was just a mild example.

He went out on the ski course, where walking was easier, and climbed upward toward the fourth level of the Hibernian, studying the ski course as he went. They had something here, all right. If the snow were any good. . . .

The route he struck above Hibernian Number Three had been a railroad grade once. Now it was a bridle path. When he reached the north side of the ski course, he plunged down through the trees and came out on one of the Vivandière dumps. Enough of it was left to tell him it was Number Three. Here most of the shed from the portal was intact. He entered it near the portal, feeling cool air bathe his face and neck.

Ninety-pound rail and concrete had been used to make the entrance solid until granite beyond the overburden held its own weight. A fast-moving stream of water ran between the tie-ends and the footwall. He stood in the damp coolness of the old bore for several moments, looking at his own tracks. They were the only ones that had disturbed the layer of film for a long time.

He walked along the track to the dry-room. The shed ended in a doorway a hundred feet from the edge of the dump. Wide entrances led from the side of the shed to the first half of the dry-room, and then a narrow door led to a second compartment exactly like the first. The sole of a gum boot, some rotting overalls, and an overturned can of waste carbide lay on the floor.

The set-up had been simple and effective to check high-grading. Miners coming off shift had been required to leave their digging clothes in the first room off the shed, then pass naked to the second room where their non-work clothes were kept. When going on shift they had gone through the process in reverse. Trammers coming out with muck or ore had not been allowed outside the door of the shed; they had probably waited in the shed while highly trusted employees took the cars on out to the dump or ore bin.

No doubt existed in Sadar's mind that the job of bringing twenty-seven sacks of high grade through a set-up like this would have been next to impossible, unless there had been assistance from the top men charged with enforcing the check.

Briefly he walked through the rest of the building. Blacksmith shop, boiler room, a big steam air compressor with the brass grease cups still intact. Rats and their foulness were everywhere. The silence of years was heavy.

He went back into the sunshine. Several hundred feet down the mountain he saw a rider moving slowly up one of the ore roads. The man was hatless. When he turned his head to look up the hill, Sadar recognized him by the glint of sun on a red beard. It was Reeves. He raised one hand and waved carelessly at Sadar, then rode slowly out of sight behind a shoulder of rock.

He knows the mountains, Sadar thought. *He'll probably be checking along behind me, wherever I go. Maybe he thinks he's made a deal with me, but still he wants to find out what I'm up to.*

The voice of Tumbling River grew loud as Sadar left the bridle path to follow a blazed trail that led around the shoulder of the mountain. Spruce began to replace aspens. Then, as he kept climbing, he heard the roar of Tumbling River growing fainter. Silvertip spruce increased in size, throwing shadows along the damp trail where his footfalls made little sound. Gloom and quiet held sway in the forest; the sounds of motors on the highway far below were only faint drones. Now and then his passing alarmed a blue squirrel, or a tattletale jay gave hoarse notice of his presence.

A half hour later he saw a break in the tree line as if he was nearing the top of a hill or a clearing.

His heart bucketed, and he stopped quickly. Ahead of him

in the trail crouched a lion, its tail a-switch, its summer brown body a stark, living contrast to the dark forest around it. Sadar stepped back without really intending to. In response, the lion's heavy shoulder muscles rippled as it took two noiseless steps toward the man. Its belly remained close to the ground, its entire muscular body following the point of its sloping head. Sadar shifted his eyes to the break in the tree line for just an instant. A thin drift of smoke was rising above the treetops.

Recalling that Jackie had told him Tarwater kept a pet lion, he steeled himself and walked forward boldly, calling: "Here, boy!"

After Sadar's third step, the lion broke, leaped sidewise into the timber, and went bounding like a mink toward the clearing.

Sunlight washed the open space Sadar reached a few minutes later. A long, rectangular cabin sat solid on a rock foundation on a little rise that faced the river a hundred yards away. Here Tumbling River moved quietly over sand and gravel. Upstream were the mud and stick walls of beaver dams. Lush grasses abounded in a field where silvertips grew sparsely. As he surveyed the clearing, he noted the sixteen-year-old pickup truck parked under a snug shed behind the cabin. Across the valley, high on the mountainside, he saw the yellow line of a road. On the far bank of the river, across a natural ford, he saw what looked like wheel ruts in the long grass. The trail he had been following continued on upstream, and passed a hundred feet or more from the cabin.

Before Sadar had a chance to approach the dwelling any closer, Sim Tarwater came out of the cabin, carrying a longbow and, slung on one shoulder, a quiver of red, untanned cowhide. Tarwater rested one end of the bow on the ground. He stood silently, his chin resting on the other end of the bow just above his scarred hand.

"Hello, Mister Tarwater."

"Hello, young Sam."

They stared at each other, Sadar uncertain as to how to begin asking what he wanted to know. In the bright light he could see a map of lines on Tarwater's face that he hadn't seen before, and he read again that same restless, uneasy look in the dark blue eyes staring out at him.

"Going to kill a deer?" he finally asked. He realized how inane the question must have been, but Tarwater gave him no time to reflect upon it.

"I haven't killed a deer in more than forty years." The strangely soothing voice hinted at much unsaid.

Two half-grown conies emerged from a break in the rock foundation. They came boldly until they saw Sadar, then the rabbits scampered between Tarwater's feet, peering around his legs like timid children. Soon they began to dig vigorously in his rolled-up overall bottoms. Tarwater was utterly still and quiet. As Sadar watched the antics of the two rabbits, his attention was drawn by a jerking activity inside Sim's shirt. Before he was able to comment, a striped chipmunk, a bold, fat critter if there ever was one, appeared suddenly on Tarwater's shoulder. Upon seeing Sadar, it jerked its tail up and down in rhythm with its squeaks and disappeared once again down Tarwater's shirt.

"I suppose you know I'm trying to find that calaverite?" Sadar said.

Sim nodded. His eyes were quiet for an instant. "Everybody has . . . for years, now."

"My grandfather didn't tell me. . . ."

He didn't know," Tarwater said quickly. "Nobody knows anything about it any more."

"That's not what I. . . ."

"I set great store by Sam," Tarwater said wistfully. "You look just like him. How much do you weigh?"

Sadar told him. "Look, Mister Tarwater, I'd like to talk about that robbery. For myself . . . that is, as far as the calaverite itself, I don't want. . . ." All the years of fighting against uncertainty and bitterness came back to Sadar. He cursed himself for stumbling. If he could only explain his quest, make Tarwater understand why he wanted to find the high grade.

"Sam done well, I hear, after he left," Tarwater said. "Mining is a dirty game, though. It's nothing but trouble." His eyes flashed wildly.

"I want to clear up . . . ," Sadar began.

"Get out of here," Tarwater said suddenly, without raising his voice.

For a breath Sadar thought the order had been directed at him. But then he understood, as he watched Tarwater stoop and disengage one of the conies that was trying to crawl inside one leg of his overalls. He pulled the little animal loose. It chittered in rage and began to chase its companion around and between Tarwater's ankles. "Darned whistle pigs!" he said mildly. He whisked an arrow from the quiver and tapped the animals lightly on their rumps. They scooted for their hole under the cabin. Sim replaced the arrow. "I got to go now. Make yourself to home in the cabin, if you want to."

"I want to find out. . . ."

"All lies, nothing but lies. Forget the whole thing." Tarwater started for the woods behind the cabin. "Make yourself to home, young Sam. Glad to have you."

Sadar battled exasperation as he watched the little man walk away. Before Tarwater reached the beginning of the forest, the lion Sadar had seen down the trail came scratching down the trunk of a tree and flowed into the woods ahead of the archer.

"Hell!" Sadar said to himself, experiencing a strong urge to run after Sim but knowing better. The words of the little man came back to him as he stood staring into the dancing shadows caused by the breeze in the tall trees: *I set great store by Sam.* "Then why won't you help me?" Sadar said out loud. But Sim and the lion were gone.

So Sim wasn't hunting deer. Yet the wooden shaft with which he had tapped the conies was tipped with a broad head, and, when Tarwater had leaned over to pull the cony loose, Sadar had seen several aluminum-shafted arrows in the quiver.

A camp robber bird lit on a chopping block at one end of the cabin. It twisted its head at Sadar, and, when Sadar walked to the cabin door, it flew to the roof. Feeling too much like a trespasser, Sadar decided against having a look-see inside. Still he couldn't help noticing the heavy wooden bar that was, oddly, on the outside of the door. His eyes scanned the cabin's exterior, noticing absently that wooden bars had been installed on the insides of the windows, as he stood debating whether to go back to Sylvanite or wait until Tarwater returned and tackle him again.

"Damn it!" he hissed, and kicked at the door. Having been warned about Sim's touchiness, he'd still opened the vug subject as abruptly as he'd tackled his grandfather—and with about the same results. He stood indecisively for several moments, studying the odd bar outside the door. Near the point where the free end dropped into an iron latch, a small passage, approximately six inches square, led in through the wall.

He decided there was no point in sticking around, since there was no telling how long Tarwater might be gone. He'd scared him off so badly perhaps it would be best to wait another day before attempting a more gentle approach. If he could only get Sim to sit still long enough to hear the whole story.

Besides, time was getting away. He'd spent too much of it in sparring. Now that everyone knew who he was and why he was in Sylvanite, why not approach the subject head-on? He thought of Reeves, wondering if the red-bearded man had followed him to the cabin. It was too bad Rouvière had broken up the conversation with Reeves just about the time it had been getting interesting.

Sadar started rapidly down the trail.

Less than a hundred yards from the cabin he met Jack Ralston. The garage man was carrying an aluminum fishing rod case and had a creel on his shoulder. Sadar looked at his low-cut street shoes and then flashed to the deep water and marshy ground in the beaver dams.

"Going to nail a few big ones?" Sadar asked.

Ralston nodded and gave him a surly look.

"You like to wade in street shoes?"

"If I do, it's my business!"

They measured each other. Ralston's look reminded Sadar of the unwavering glint he'd seen in the lion's eyes only a short time before, near this exact spot.

"Another thing that isn't your business, Sadar, is poking around the Hibernian tunnels. I saw you on the dump at Number Six."

"You don't object to a person's walking across your property, do you?"

The sneer lines became channels in Ralston's cheeks. "Tell your boss . . . tell Rouvière he'd better keep his stooges away from the Hibernian."

Ralston went around Sadar and continued walking up the

trail. The flat grips of an automatic pistol showed between the blue steel butt frame of a gun in his hip pocket.

Sadar went down the trail, wondering why Ralston was so sure the calaverite was in the Hibernian. At that, he considered, the Hibernian was the most logical place for the sacks to be. Ralston had tried to get Rouvière interested in the proposition, then had turned sour when Rouvière refused. Now, it seemed, Ralston was convinced that Rouvière had sent Sadar to buy the mine.

Chapter Nine

NO GAME FOR PIKERS

The receptionist in Reeves's office told Sadar that Reeves was not in. "Mister Rouvière is, though," she added.

"He'll do," Sadar snapped.

The chain of command went to work, and presently Pete Dill beckoned Sadar from the door to the inside office.

The millionaire seemed to fit Reeves's desk better than the owner. He watched Sadar cross the room, and then nodded toward a chair. More than ever Sadar noticed the contrast between the man's mild eyes and hammer-like jaw.

Sadar sat down, wondering how far he ought to go in revealing Reeves's underhanded deal. Rouvière sat quietly, still watching. Then a smile blossomed and faded in almost the same instant. "Any luck?" he asked.

Sadar shook his head and started talking. He told his reason for wanting to find the calaverite. Whether or not Rouvière believed the story was a moot point. He listened politely enough and didn't miss a word.

At the end of Sadar's story, Rouvière said: "I can understand and appreciate why you would want the matter cleared up, but I'm afraid it's impossible."

"Ralston doesn't seem to think so."

"Ralston had a wild theory about a cross-cut far back on

the fifth level of Hibernian, but it would cost a fortune to get to it," Rouvière explained.

"I understand you once considered re-opening the Vivandière?"

Rouvière ran one hand over the sheen of his bald head. "I did, but a conservative estimate of costs changed my mind in a hurry. The calaverite will never be found."

"You don't think my grandfather . . . ?"

"I do not! It may interest you to know that many years ago I had the source of your grandfather's income investigated thoroughly."

Sadar stared into Rouvière's eyes. They were as gentle as a bloodhound's, but the area below the man's mouth and jaw was as harsh as the blunt face of a maul.

"My uncle turned that hill inside out to find that calaverite," Rouvière stated. "The workings were accessible then. But think what they might be like now."

"Maybe he overlooked something," Sadar said.

Rouvière's lower lip went dubious. "Very unlikely."

The man seemed sincere. Sadar wondered if he knew that Reeves had added another employee in a deal that was in direct opposition to Rouvière's attitude toward the missing calaverite.

"Did you know your manager hired me?"

Rouvière's jaw was truly grim now. "What for?"

"Ski instructor next winter, odd jobs during the summer."

Rouvière digested the information slowly. His voice was crisp when he spoke. "As of now, consider yourself discharged. I'll instruct Dill to give you a check for two weeks salary."

"What's the reason?"

"Two reasons," Rouvière said briskly. "First, it would be poor business policy to pay you for odd jobs until winter.

Second, I'm inclined to think you may have got Reeves worked up over that calaverite story. I want my employees to concentrate on necessary work, not some hopeless treasure hunt." Rouvière's heavy jaw snapped shut, and he sat looking politely at Sadar.

The reasons, Sadar thought, were quite logical. "Forget the check for two weeks," he suggested.

"I prefer to pay it."

Sadar thought of the old men at the Fire Horse Club. They could use the money, if Rouvière wanted to be stiff-necked. "Suit yourself," he said.

He paused at the door to take one last look at the millionaire, trying vainly to find some other reason for being fired, other than the two perfectly plausible ones given. Rouvière's face was expressionless. His neatly trimmed fringe of brown hair looked like a band of rich velvet below the hard, metallic gleam of his bald head. His large, polite eyes rested unblinkingly on Sadar, and below was that brutal jaw and nutcracker mouth set in hard composure.

"Good bye, Mister Sadar," Rouvière said.

A half hour later Sadar was headed for the forlorn part of town that held the Fire Horse Club. In his pocket was one hundred and eighty dollars of unearned money from Rouvière's check. He didn't like the feel of it and wanted to get rid of it as soon as possible.

It struck him that a minor puzzling aspect of his talk with Rouvière was the implication that the millionaire did not trust Reeves's judgment in relation to the high grade. Maybe Rouvière didn't trust Reeves's honesty, either, but he wasn't doing anything about it. Sadar considered what the farmer had told him about Reeves's dishonest invoices. Well, that was Rouvière's problem.

He saw the Fire Horse ahead, its clean windows standing out among the surrounding structures with boarded fronts, broken windows, and dusty entrances. Maybe deep-voiced old Ben Liggett would suspect that Sadar was trying to bribe him into enlarging his warning when Sadar offered to donate the money to the club.

Upon his arrival Sadar found he would have to wait to find out how Ben would respond because the bartender was not in the club. Its only occupants were the Swede and three others who were playing poker in the casino. Except that the Swede had changed his white shirt for a blue one, already rumpled enough for three days' wearing, he appeared to have been sitting in the same chair all night. He greeted Sadar jovially. The other players grunted briefly, looking annoyed by the interruption.

"Where's Ben?" Sadar asked.

"On the crank at Deedee's shaft," one of the players said curtly. "Deal up, Jammer," he told the Swede.

Sadar watched for several moments. "All profits of this game go to the club?" he inquired.

The Swede grinned at his companion. "Every damn' cent goes to the house!"

"Every cent," a player repeated.

The man in front of Sadar drew to three tens after the player under the gun opened. The Swede dealt two queens to go with the tens. Betting ran heavy. The Swede laid down his hand and yawned. A third player stayed, running several stacks of pale yellow chips and a flush hard against the full house. He read the sad news with a grunt.

"Under the gun I open, with three fat K-boys," the loser muttered. "He draws two lousy cards and fills!"

Sadar took the one hundred and eighty dollars from his wallet. He dropped the notes on the table. "Who's the bank?"

Three of the players looked at each other quietly, then at the Swede, who picked the money up slowly. "This all you want?"

Sadar nodded.

The Swede reached down on the floor and came up with three white chips. There wasn't another one on the table. All four players looked at Sadar with expressionless faces. He met their questioning stares, and a feeling of utter foolishness began to make his forehead hot.

Sixty dollars for a white chip! The ante was one blue. The yellows must be worth five hundred or a thousand.

The Swede started to stow the money in a wallet heavy with other notes. "I'll stake you for a hundred and twenty, and you can play one hand for the ante." His little eyes arched inquiringly at Sadar.

Sadar took another look at the wooden faces of the other players. His voice didn't seem to come out as it should when he said: "Maybe I'm getting over my head. Forget it."

The Swede handed the money back. "Always like to have new blood in our little game."

Sadar tried a grin. "That isn't blood . . . it's murder!"

The Swede laughed.

"Whose deal?" one of the players asked impatiently.

Sadar went out of the casino with the back of his head burning. He felt that derisive grins were following him all the way, but, when he turned suddenly and looked back, all four men were completely intent on their game.

He stood a moment at the end of the bar, his thoughts awash from the impact of the high-stake game. Were they ribbing him? They had to be. He glanced at the empty bottles on the back-bar, and thought of Ducray's patched shirt. Another quick glance behind him showed that no one was paying him the least attention. If they were acting, they ought to have

Academy Awards. The words of Ducray came back to him: *A few of us old-timers try to stick together the best way we can.* The best seemed very good, indeed, what with white chips at sixty bucks a head and none in the game. With money like that around, what business had Ben and Ducray up on the hill working a shallow hole?

He looked toward the players again in an attempt to catch a grin being thrown his way. They didn't seem to know he was there. Some game, he thought, if the Swede's words were on the level. He felt fast-rising curiosity about the kind of mine Ducray and Ben were working on top of the hill. He toyed with the idea of going to have a look for himself, but decided it was too late in the day to be starting up there. But tomorrow. . . .

When Sadar returned to the Fire Horse after dinner, Ben was sacked out, snoring like a fat bear. The poker game was going strong, with a few new hands in addition to some of the others from the afternoon session. The Swede invited Sadar to sit in with such heartiness that Sadar's suspicion of having been ribbed came back. No one smiled.

Not wanting to wake Ben, Sadar headed off to Ducray's shack. The place was dark. He considered knocking, but thought better of it, figuring that, like Ben, Ducray had turned in for the night.

Walking back to the hotel, he vowed he'd have a look at the old boys' mine first thing in the morning. As he neared Ralston's garage, he saw Charley stationed on the automobile cushions out front. They talked briefly about the weather before Sadar asked Charley if he knew a fellow named Jammer, the name used by one of the players in the poker game in addressing the Swede.

"Jammer Roos? Hell, yes! Haven't seen Jammer for six,

seven months, I reckon. Where'd you play poker with him?"
Old Charley cackled at the implication.

"Saw him in Phoenix or Los Angeles or some place,"
Sadar made up quickly, mulling over the fact that the Swede,
this Jammer Roos, apparently was hiding out at the Fire
Horse Club.

"That's where he winters, sure enough!" Charley said.

As they engaged in more small talk, Sadar wondered about
the implications of the clandestine presence of Jammer at the
casino.

Early the next morning Sadar started up the mountain.
This time he followed the railroad grade for a long way, de-
touring at three rotting trestles where they made long switch-
backs. Above Number Five Vivandière he started taking short
cuts straight up the slope. Above Number Two Vivandière,
far up the mountain, he again encountered the bridle path.
The way ahead, he noticed, seemed oddly bare of vegetation.
When he got to the point where the grade intersected the line
of the Vivandière tunnel, he saw the reason.

The roadbed was made of concrete reinforced with steel
rails, and spanned an enormous hole. Sloping sides, where
trees were rooted, led down and down to darkness.
Weathered rocks, still gripped between the closely placed re-
inforcements, showed that the bridge had once rested on
both sides of a lesser cave-in, for a cave-in it was, a collapsed
stope that had run almost to the surface. He tossed a large
rock up and out. It turned slowly, with the sun reflecting
brightly on the mica, and flashed downward past the aspens
clinging to the sloping sides. Seconds later Sadar heard the
ca-choom! of the stone striking water somewhere far below.

He followed the path that detoured on the upper side and
continued on the grade until he saw that it was not going to
lead him upward very fast. Knowing that Ducray's claim lay

athwart the ski course on top of the mountain, he cut through the trees on an angling course calculated to bring him close to it.

It wasn't long before he came across a mine dump that was much smaller than most of the waste piles on Sylvan Mountain. Water was working its way from a caved portal and had undermined one side of a decrepit blacksmith's shop. As he started to pass above the portal, he stopped suddenly, staring at the fresh tracks that disappeared down a slanting hole between the tunnel roof and the muck pile. From the long gouges in the slope it appeared that someone had scrambled in and out of that hole recently. He looked on the uphill side at the shattered rocks thrown to the surface years before, when the first cut had been made to start the tunnel. The rocks were resting precariously in the dry dirt, posed, ready to start a miniature run with very little urging. But someone had ventured into the opening.

Made nervous by the precariousness of the setting, Sadar let himself down gingerly, careful not to disturb the uphill balance of rocks and dirt. Notwithstanding, when he slipped on some loose dirt, he grabbed at an upended piece of pole lagging. Cork-light from dry rot, the wood broke, and he sat down hard on the sloping muck. Fine dust filtered down in a dry stream, causing him to hold his breath, but the rocks above him didn't move. He eased himself on down to the tunnel floor and stood up.

A swarm of gnats hovering just beyond the light brushed against his face and attempted to nest in his brows. He brushed at the pesky insects, feeling coolness from the bore wash over him. Once his eyes became accustomed to the gloom ahead, he saw that big sections of decomposing granite had sloughed from the walls, half choking the tunnel. He walked a few paces ahead hesitantly. A dark sheen of still water lay beyond the barrier. *Nothing,* he reflected, *is as black and motionless as water trapped underground.*

Examining the ground, he identified a series of rather small footprints, proof that someone had preceded him into the hole, looked at the bore ahead, and, sensibly, had gone back to safe sunlight.

He decided to do the same. But before he could move, rocks and dirt began to slide. In small amounts, at first. Then it seemed that all the mass of loose material above the opening had broken away. It poured down rapidly, causing Sadar's heart to palpitate as he froze rooted to the ground. When the slide ceased, Sadar still remained stationary, beads of perspiration having erupted from nearly every pore on his body. The smell of dust and dry rot assaulted his nostrils as he squinted at the small shafts of light coming through openings no thicker than his hand at the tunnel entrance.

Stay out of old holes, 'lessin you're figuring on timbering up! Sadar recalled the advice of a veteran miner. *Then start from the surface and do your work sound.*

Sadar looked at the barrier, reflecting how wonderful and futile good advice is. He had no illusion about his predicament. Move one rock, another comes down to take its place. Move that one. . . . Keep on moving rocks.

He sat down on the slope of muck, postponing for the time the seven different kinds of fools he was going to call himself. The mine was no longer cool. It was cold and damp.

Soon he realized the sounds of water gurgling in the rocks had disappeared. He looked down. The water was backing up behind the new cave-in that had contained enough fine material to choke the existing outlets among the rocks. Well, it would only go so high before it found new outlets or washed the old ones clear, but it might go high enough to make a man rather unhappy, especially if it got neck-deep. Feeling an added urgency, he went to work, dragging loose rocks away from the muck pile, letting those above tumble down, alert at all times for any large round stones that might come bounding down to break a leg or crush a foot. Although he was far from panicking, he knew that the rocks he threw in the water behind him contributed to its rising level, and that his feet, churning on the sides of the slope, helped pack the fine material hard to form a tighter dam.

It wasn't long before he had made a small opening, even if rock-edged and ready to grind shut any minute. Sadar grasped the long piece of dry lagging that had broken during his descent and poked it carefully through the hole, probing for big rocks around the outside of the opening. He found one, and immediately pulled back. A sigh escaped his lips. He felt a brief moment of relief, for he hadn't exerted much pressure with the rotten post, but, before another second had passed, he knew the rock had a hair-trigger temper. The rock came slamming down just as Sadar leaped back. Others followed. The settling of the dust revealed that, now, the opening was even smaller and jammed with bigger stones than he remembered having been above the portal. And the water was numbing cold around his ankles.

Chapter Ten

WAITING GAME

If Rigdon Sadar had inherited anything from his grandfather besides a huge frame and a resemblance that Sam Rigdon's old friends had recognized instantly, it was a tendency toward cool-headedness under pressure.

He sat on the slope of muck just inside the portal of the tunnel for which he didn't even have a name. He scowled at the broken piece of lagging beside him and tried to think calmly. Maybe those rocks had slid by themselves. Their hold on the hill had been slight. He wondered who the other fool had been who had recently preceded him into the tunnel. That idiot had been luckier—he had gotten out again.

Water began to suck near his feet. That's what he had been waiting for, a sound that meant water had begun to melt away the fine material clogging passage through the rocks. If he didn't trample about on the muck pile, tamping the particles into crevices with his big feet, the water would give him no trouble. But sitting still wouldn't gain him his freedom, wouldn't remove that jam of rocks, even though trying to move them might bring down a roller from which he couldn't get his legs away. But someone outside could unblock the entrance without much work or danger.

Very good, Sadar berated himself, *all I have to do is wait for someone to come by . . . next month or next year.* He shoved the rotten lagging that had fallen near him. He tried to comfort himself, as he settled in to wait, with the thought that it wasn't far to the bridle path above.

The hours went slowly, while he beat down a growing urge to get up and start tearing at the barrier with his hands. In a short time he'd have to try, he knew.

Then he heard voices outside. He shouted. The words ran hollowly in the bore, rolled around him, and died quickly. At first, in response, there was silence outside, then rock clattered, and the light was shut off completely.

"What are you doing down there?" a woman's voice called out.

"I was born here!" he yelled back.

"Oh!" He heard laughter, heard talk he couldn't understand. Then the voice came once more. "In that case, you won't mind it down there a little longer. Stay back!"

He waited in knee-deep icy water. Rocks bounced down the slope, splashing water on him. Soon ends of boards showed through a growing opening. He could hear his rescuers laugh and joke, occasionally shouting down to inquire if he were still there.

When the opening was big enough to allow the passing of a human body, Sadar scrambled up the slope, and, clawing his way free of the rocks, was greeted by the smile of Jackie Rouvière.

She extended one hand to him to help him gain his balance amongst the rubble of rocks and the blinding sunshine. With the other, she held out a flask, saying: "You could probably use some of this. Cheers!"

Uncertain as to what to say, Sadar blinked at her, feeling foolish as he accepted the flask and took a small sip. Off to the side, chubby Myra, the beard-yanking conspirator, was standing with a board in her hands. Two horses on the dump pricked their ears toward him.

"Thanks," he finally said.

Jackie brushed her hands together and frowned. "Well, that'll have to do for now. But it's going to cost you more than that for afflicting me with abandoned-mine hands." She laughed, grabbed the flask from Sadar's hand, and took a healthy gulp. "What on earth were you doing down there?" she asked.

"I got to chasing a rabbit so fast I couldn't stop."

Myra giggled, the vibration running to all parts of her body. "Jackie heard your yelling. I would have ridden right on past, little knowing that we had a man trapped and at our mercy."

"I have an investigative mind," Jackie said. "By the way, did you catch the rabbit?"

"It got away." Sadar grinned, then glanced at the uphill slope. Lying near the portal where the rocks had started sliding was a dead aspen, recently torn from the ground. Mold still clung to the root stubs. "I guess that tree came in handy . . . for pushing the rocks," Sadar said.

Jackie's eyes followed Sadar's line of vision. She shook her head, her attention now drawn to his face. "We didn't even see it until after we tore a couple of boards off that old shack."

The aspen hadn't been there before he went into the hole. The girls hadn't used it, according to Jackie. But someone had—to start the slide?

He heard the sound of a horse on the bridle path. Jackie turned and shouted: "Biff! Up here!" She explained Biff's presence to Sadar: "Biff rode out ahead of us to look at a lodge site on top of the hill. We got tired of waiting where he was supposed to meet us at Number Zero Viv."

Sadar glanced at the aspen again and, out of the corner of

his eye, caught Jackie's gaze following his up the slope. As Reeves approached, Sadar had to allow that he rode well as he watched the red-bearded man work his horse up the steep pitch below the dump. Reeves was wearing faded dungarees, short boots with logger heels, and a plaid shirt. Every hair on his head seemed to be in place, and his beard was shining. He dismounted on the dump, his brown eyes taking in the scene alertly.

"This looks like quite a party," he commented, brushing a tuft of leaves from his pants. "I'll bet there hasn't been so many people on the old Commander dump since Nineteen Ten."

"Seems sense has finally descended upon Sylvanite," Jackie stated, then added in an undertone: "Although it's a little too late for some of us."

After that cryptic comment Sadar reminded himself that he needed to get back to Ben Liggett for that story on Jackie. In the meantime, he now knew the name of this particular site. His attention was drawn to Reeves as his face changed perceptibly when Jackie began to explain what had happened. Something in Reeves's face, when he glanced at him, told Sadar that Rouvière had made no secret about his firing Reeves's latest hire. By the time Jackie had finished the story, Reeves was studying Sadar from head to foot, and his look indicated that he had dismissed Sadar, as if he had been weighed and found light. The strong dislike Sadar had read in the other's eyes, even when Reeves was trying to be pleasant with his underhanded proposal, was back in force now.

He figures I don't know what the hell I'm doing, Sadar reflected. *And he's right, what's more. From now on I'm right back on that well-known list of his.* He wondered again if Reeves knew anything about the calaverite, or whether he had been edging toward an unholy alliance to find out what Sadar knew.

"Did you *build* that lodge while you were up the mountain, Biff?" Myra interjected into the silence that had fallen among the group.

Reeves jerked himself away from some obviously unpleasant considerations. A smile washed smoothly across his face as he addressed Jackie, ignoring Myra and her question. "I'm sorry I held you up. I cruised a little timber while I was up there and sort of forgot how late it was getting. That site I picked has everything!" He busied himself in a description of several natural advantages overlooked by the world for years.

Sadar wondered how the mountain had got along all this time without Reeves.

While Biff carried on enthusing about his choice in sites, Jackie turned her face toward the sun, closing her eyes and appearing, to Sadar, as if she was drawing energy from the warming rays. Each encounter with her peaked his curiosity to know more, to understand. She was an amalgam of emotions—carefree, spontaneous, fearless, and, at times, wistful, distant, maybe even sad. Her interactions with the men at the Fire Horse Club indicated she was accepted as "one of the boys," despite her blood connection to the top man in Sylvanite. And what about her fondness for alcohol? For what weakness had it become a crutch? Sadar was brought back to the present by the voice of this woman of mystery.

"I'm supposed to meet Dad for dinner, and, if I don't hurry up, I'll have to pay the price. So-o-o . . . we'd better get to getting." She looked at Sadar. "Need a horse to ride down, or are you oblivious to your harrowing ordeal of ninety-nine hours in an old mine with neither food nor companionship?"

Sadar grinned. "Shortest ninety-nine hours I've ever spent. Besides, the beauty and charm of my rescuers made it all worthwhile." Myra gasped and clutched at the nape of her neck. Sadar smiled at Jackie's companion, and continued, addressing both young women: "So, no. No more assistance is needed at the present time. I thought I'd head up toward Ducray's mine, anyway."

Reeves cleared his throat and shook his head. "They're not there now. They were when I rode up, but they were gone when I came back."

For a fleeting moment Sadar was struck by the thought that either Ben or Ducray could have shoved the rocks down into the Commander portal. Dismissing the idea as nonsense, he instead studied Reeves carefully, wondering if Reeves had mentioned their absence from the mine with the calculated idea of planting a suspicion of guilt on them.

Reeves looked back coldly, his expression plainly saying: *You're no good to me, Sadar.*

"If you *have* to go calling on people, you can always slip around the mountain and see that little man . . . Tarwater," Myra said. "Jackie tells me you think she ought to give Biff-Biff back to him," she added irrelevantly, and began blushing as Sadar's gaze stayed on her.

"I may go see him, at that," Sadar responded lightly, sensing her discomfort and trying to alleviate it.

"Don't stay after dark," Jackie called as she swung up onto her horse. "The lion, you know." She glanced carelessly at the aspen pole, then rode off the dump.

Sadar listened to the thump of the hoofs as the trio rode away. He took off his shoes, wrang out his socks, and laid them to dry for a while in the sun. As he sat there, it came to him that he'd been downright lucky to get out of the hole without a broken leg. For the first time since having been rescued he had the full opportunity to give way to the expansive feeling that can come over a man by just walking into fresh air and sunshine after a shift underground.

As he surveyed the landscape, his eyes fell once again on

the aspen lying above the portal. So it appeared that this was the second time someone had tried to slow him down, and, although the attempt had not been as much of a dangerous threat as had been the arrow from the dark, perhaps it had been the best opportunity available to his nemesis. He probably could have gotten out of the tunnel by himself, but at some risk of a broken leg, to be sure. And whoever had caused the slide must have known that. This incident seemed to be more of a warning than a deliberate attempt to kill him. That made it seem as though the rockslide had been started by someone other than the person who had tried to whisk the broad-head arrow through his belly, unless the slide had been a spur-of-the-moment notion. At any rate, it was the result of his own foolishness and someone else's grasping of a handy opportunity.

Sadar's mind flashed to the tracks and the person who had made them. Why and what would someone be investigating in such a dangerous place? "And what about yourself then?" he said aloud. He retrieved his socks, and, after putting on his shoes, he walked over to have a look at Reeves's tracks. He found the heel marks were deep and clean-cut. Above the portal, after a careful examination, he found there were no marks similar to the ones Reeves had made. The culprit, who-ever it had been, hadn't disturbed even the mat of humus and undergrowth in reaching out with the pole to get the rocks to moving. He studied the aspen. In several places the root stubs showed dents from having been jammed hard against stone. Sadar continued his search, prowling around in the trees until he found the place where the aspen had been torn from the soil.

"You're a great detective," Sadar mumbled to himself. "After something happens, you can find evidence that it hap-pened . . . but that's about all.

As he continued his haphazard search over the area, looking for any kind of clue, he went back over his two days in Sylvanite, evaluating what he'd thus far accomplished. Arriving without any sort of plan, because he'd lacked information from the very start, he'd worked thus far on a hit-and-miss basis, trying to cover any and every angle that had come up. He'd made only one stride—that someone else, perhaps knowing the whereabouts of the calaverite, felt that Sadar's very presence was a threat.

Many of the puzzling things he'd encountered—the endless, uncertain poker game at the Fire Horse; Reeves's crookedness and his quick change of attitude toward Sadar; Sim Tarwater's personal history—all might have some sort of bearing on the high grade. The attempt to kill him with the arrow certainly must, and several other incidents, including the recent rockslide, but, if he tried to clear them all up individually, he'd be getting nowhere. Eventually the pattern might take shape, but, in the meantime, his seven days would be gone. He'd already wasted enough time. Even if he concentrated on finding the person who had tried to kill him and found him, that individual wouldn't automatically tell him anything about the calaverite. He was going to have to follow a straight line, one step at a time. So far, the most promising lead he had was Sim Tarwater.

With no specific plan in mind, Sadar went as fast as he could toward Tarwater's cabin. But as his luck would have it, the little man was not at home. The conies came out of their retreat, looked him over, and then retired in haste. Several chipmunks ran along the walls and chittered at him as he stood at the open door, looking inside. Less than half of the cabin had been given to living quarters; the rest held a woodworking shop, including a lathe powered by a gasoline motor. Sitting in a cleared space was a completed porch seat made of aspen and cedar, the red and white of the cedar wood shining so brightly Sadar knew that it must have been covered with clear varnish only a short time before. All the windows were covered with a latticework of light wooden bars. That Sim encouraged no overnight visitors was evident from the fact that there was only one single bed in the room.

He shut the door, looking more curiously on this visit at the outside bar from which a piece of clothesline rope led through a hole in the planking. In Sim's case the old gag about the latchstring was reversed. Sadar stooped to peer into the square opening through the logs near the free end of the bar. The small passage was blocked midway by a swinging door, a neat barrier that swung outward only, he discovered, when he poked at it with his fingers. Sadar gave it up as a Tarwater peculiarity, and headed for the shed.

The pickup truck, he discovered, had two flat tires. They had been that way so long that the ground under them was damp. Next, he wandered over to the ford that crossed Tumbling River. Tire marks of recent origin showed in the grassy bank on the near side. Apparently there was a road of some sort from the cabin to the yellow slash that marked the highway cut on the mountain a mile beyond.

He sat down on the chopping block and waited. After an hour he had made friends with two chipmunks, one of which was the fat one that had run up Tarwater's back. He waited some more.

Light was retreating from the grassy meadows up the creek, the silvertips were turning blue, and trout were beginning to feed on insects along the shallow edges of the beaver ponds when he decided to wait no longer. He admitted to himself freely that he didn't care to walk back down the trail in the dark. He wondered if Sim had spotted him from the edge of the trees and was just waiting for him to leave.

Tarwater would know there was only one reason for his being here—and Tarwater didn't want to discuss that reason.

In light of what Ben had told him of Tarwater's experience after the robbery, Sadar could respect his desire not to be reminded of the old days. But Tarwater's life was behind him, Sadar's was ahead, and he didn't want it to be forever troubled by old ghosts, false though they were. Freedom from the past was something Tarwater had tried to attain by running away from people. The haunted uneasiness of his eyes was proof that the effort had not been successful. Tarwater would understand, Sadar felt sure. But first he had to be cornered.

He waited until dusk, then started down the back trail. At the edge of the timber he looked back, hoping to see Tarwater appear. The cabin remained lonely and gloomy, and the trees seemed to have moved in closer toward it.

He ate dinner at the Big Stope, surprised to find the food not nearly as bad as he had expected. He was *not* surprised to find he owed $2.50 for a small steak. If Reeves was free-handed in spending Rouvière's money, he was also careful about gathering in more of it to spend. Well, what with tourist season in full bloom and Boom Days in the offing. . . .

He stopped at the desk in the lobby to chat with Al Harris, reading in the clerk's expression that he would welcome a chance to talk about Sadar's mission. Terry and Gary temporarily gave up their slugging of each other to listen to Sadar and watch him with great interest. He felt they were scanning his pockets for evidence of bulges that would betray success.

"Anybody still living around here who worked at the Vivandière when the vug was tapped?" Sadar asked. "Besides Sim Tarwater, I mean."

Al shook his head. "Not a soul that I know of. There's a

few old-timers who claim to know all about it, now that so much time has passed, but, when you try to pin 'em down, you find they never really worked at the Viv at all . . . on any of the levels."

"I bet *you've* even stirred around a little after that calaverite?" Sadar ribbed Harris.

Al grinned. "When I was a kid, I put in my shift shambling around old diggings looking for it."

"Hey, I even had a look around this very morning!" Terry or Gary said. "I was in a lot of places!"

Sadar looked at the duo of bellhops. "Including the Commander?" he asked, failing to keep the edge out of his voice.

The bellhops stared at each other.

"Where the blacksmith's shop was leaning way over to one side toward the ditch?" Sadar prompted.

"Yeah!" the boys said together. "But I wouldn't crawl down in that old place!" one of them added.

That's great, Sadar thought. *I stuck my neck out to follow the tracks of a curious kid.* He began warning both bellhops about going into old diggings, advice that he knew wouldn't be heeded. It was the glaze settling over the two sets of eyes that told Sadar his lecture was going a little limp. By their expressions Terry and Gary had considered it a waste of time from the first word.

Sadar shrugged, and turned back to Al. "How about Ducray and Ben Liggett? Where'd they work?"

"My old man told me Deedee was at the Digman mine most of his career. Liggett was a railroad engineer, I think."

"Railroad engineer," Sadar repeated as he watched Terry and Gary initiate their latest display of horsing around as they tried to snap each other's lone suspender. "Was Rouvière around this morning?" Sadar asked the desk clerk.

"I assume he was riding on the mountain. He does almost

every day, generally in the morning."

One of the bellhops nudged Sadar. "Hey, will you carry me by the seat of my pants . . . like you did him," nodding toward his twin.

Sadar grinned at Al, shaking his head, and then winked. He scooped up both boys, one in each hand, by the slack of their pants and carried them across the lobby to the mine car. There he dumped them inside. They were delighted and immediately tried to tip the car over. "I'll beat you to the loot yet!" one of them cried as Sadar started out the door.

He stopped to hold the door for Mrs. Mahogany who was on her way inside. She beamed her thanks, looked at Terry and Gary struggling in the car, and set herself for a conversation. "Oh, Mister Rigdon!" she cried. "Isn't youth wonderful? Such delightfully vital boys! They remind me. . . ."

Sadar bowed. "Thank you, madam!" he said, as if taking all earthly credit for Terry and Gary. He left her slightly uncollected and went out.

Upon his arrival at The Fire Horse Club, Sadar found it not only dark, but locked. In the gloom of night the building lost its inhabited identity and seemed to revert easily to the air of decay that characterized all the other structures near it, as if it had struggled too long to remain aloof from comrades falling into ruin.

Sadar's next attempt to locate one of the old-timers, proved just as fruitless, for he could hear snoring emanate from Ducray's shack before he opened the wire gate. The sounds were fearful when he stood by an open window at the side of the house. Just listening made Sadar yawn. He realized he was more exhausted from the tension of sitting in the Commander tunnel most of the day than he would have been from strenuous exertion. He closed the gate gently behind him.

Nor did he find old Charley on his throne of broken springs when he wandered to Ralston's garage. Instead, the seat was occupied by a moon-faced lad who was trying to read a comic book in the poor light from the bulbs above the pumps. He explained that Charley didn't work except when he "damned pleased," and this evening was not one of the times Charley pleased.

Not wanting to go back to his hotel room yet, Sadar stopped in the Windlass Bucket with the idea of having one drink, but turned right around when he saw there was no one in evidence with whom he cared to pass the time. Finally, he had a thin malted milk in the drugstore, where he watched a group of youngsters enjoy a free read at the magazine rack. He tried to appear interested when the druggist got rather bitter about the horrible things the East was doing to the West.

For a few minutes, in front of the hotel, Sadar watched a swarm of insects get too curious with the searing tongues of the carbide lamps and depart this world with a *sput!* that sent them into flat spins toward the walk.

Inside, Sadar was presented with the regulars. Terry and Gary were slumped in the shapes of bent automobile cranks on a leather-covered sofa, no doubt storing up energy for their next enterprise. Al had taken off his hard-boiled hat and was rubbing gently at the indented red band the webbing had left on his forehead. In a chair near one of the granite columns, a position that commanded all inlets and bayous of the lobby, Mrs. Mahogany was waiting to make a conversational power dive in someone's direction. She shifted a little and gave the impression of warming up her motor when she saw Sadar.

Key in hand, he scurried to his room. The walls seemed closer than usual, and, try as he might, Sadar could not overcome his restlessness, fueled by a feeling of tension over a day that had yielded nothing. Vainly he tried to relax and bring back the overwhelming tiredness he had felt while outside Ducray's shack. Shoes and jacket off, he lay down on the bed, trying to make scattered facts and impressions fit into some kind of a complete unit. They wouldn't jell.

In retrospect, he regretted not having asked Rouvière to see the maps of the Vivandière levels, so that he could have a clear idea of what the working near the vug had looked like forty-five years before. He was certain that would help some, but more important were the workings of the Hibernian. Fat chance, indeed, would there be to see the level maps of the Hibernian. He closed his eyes. *Fat chance. . . .* Water dripping down the shaft outside his window sent cool air into the room. He imagined he could hear the comfortable rumble of Tumbling River gnawing at rock in its cañon passage. *There sure are a lot of holes on Sylvan Mountain . . . and Pete Dill could swim right along with the salmon . . . .*

He woke at two o'clock, blinked painfully at the light, took off the rest of his clothes, and staggered headlong under the covers of his bed. In the instant before he fell asleep, as clear as a white cloud in bright sunshine, he saw the green iron Mike outside the drugstore, its water bubbling. Standing beside it and smiling at him was the grandmother he had never known.

Chapter Eleven

INDIAN IN THE BIG STOPE

The sun had not yet touched the forest floor the next morning when he approached Sim Tarwater's cabin, watching carefully for the lion as he walked. Rising smoke told him that, for the moment at least, he had Sim trapped. Now, if he could hold him long enough to keep him from taking a sudden dart into the woods. . . .

He was still fifteen feet from the door when Timwater's shout came from the inside: "Wait a minute!" His tone carried a crack of urgency Sadar hadn't heard before. "Go a ways toward the river!" he continued to yell.

Sadar obeyed, wondering if anyone ever had gotten close enough to Tarwater's cabin to knock before their presence was known to him. Then he saw Tarwater's thin face peer from the barely opened door. The planks swung wide, and Tarwater began to speak in his normal, soothing voice.

A long, brownish form flowed through the doorway. The lion saw Sadar instantly, started toward him slowly.

"Don't get excited," Tarwater said quietly. "He's just curious." He spoke to the lion without raising his voice, and the big cat stopped. It scratched the ground in a humping stretch, then went around the corner of the cabin, and disappeared into the forest. Tarwater waved Sadar inside.

"You don't keep that little playmate in here all night, do you?" Sadar asked.

Tarwater shook his head, his eyes darting over Sadar's face. "I can trust him just as far as his nature will let him be trusted. I make sure he's never in after dark." Tarwater waved Sadar toward a rawhide chair. "Had your breakfast?"

Sadar nodded.

"Want a cup of coffee?"

"No, thanks." Sadar remembered his determination not to plunge headlong into topics that would disturb Tarwater. "You seem to get along pretty good with animals," he said.

Little Sim Tarwater nodded. "You can tell what an animal will do. Take Chinook, the lion, for instance . . . he'd jump me in a second, if he got too restless from being cooped up, or if I ever hurt myself, and he got a strong whiff of fresh blood. But if those two things never happen, he'll stay with me until he's almost full grown. Then he'll walk into the woods someday and never come back, except maybe to prowl around the cabin sometimes at night, or follow way off to one side of me when I'm alone in the woods."

Sadar saw that much of the fever was gone from Tarwater's eyes. He decided to follow the animal tack for a while.

Tarwater's face relaxed, his eyes held Sadar's without darting, and, now and then, he smiled as he talked about his pets. The bars on the windows, he explained, had been put in place because the summer before he had had a pet deer that believed any light meant an exit. The curious latch arrangement was an outgrowth of a cub bear's habit of opening the door in the middle of the night, and neglecting to close it. The cub had learned to master several simple bar locks, but wound up completely baffled when Tarwater put the bar outside and left the latch inside. "He had that bar in his mind so strong he was lost when he couldn't see it, even when I tried to teach him how to pull the string from the inside."

The coppery little man confirmed Sadar's guess that the one-way swinging door in the chute near the bar was to allow egress for smaller pets but prevent their coming in to do mischief in the cabin while Tarwater was absent.

Tarwater's tension was completely gone by the time he shifted to the subject of his woodworking shop. He showed Sadar his equipment and explained that he spent a great deal of time making lawn and porch chairs for a market Deedee Ducray had developed. "Rustic chairs, the Sylvan Mountain mine, vegetable gardens . . . ," Tarwater enumerated the many ways in which Ducray had worked to keep the old-timers going.

Tarwater bobbed his head. "And, you know, he never took a cent for anything. Deedee had a little money saved, he did. When things went bad for some of us, he helped out till he was busted. Him and Ben got that club down there so any old-timer could have a place to go and sit, or go and stay. I've seen both Ben and Deedee do without clothes to help other people out. I've seen 'em go hungry and laugh about it, so's someone else could eat."

It occurred to Sadar that Ben and Ducray might have an income from some hidden source. Suppose they'd found the calaverite and, slowly, were siphoning it off as legitimate ore taken from their mine on the mountain? The thought became strong, caught fire. He'd have to check that mine as soon as possible. In the meantime, Tarwater was talking so naturally Sadar decided to try to bring him around to the subject of the robbery, gently. Maybe if he let Tarwater run on, the little man might bring the subject up without direction. It was a lot to hope for, but he was encouraged by the steadiness of Tarwater's eyes.

So he listened to Tarwater explain an oil treatment to prevent native cedar from drying out and cracking, and the way to slant dowel holes for maximum strength when using aspen wood. Sadar nodded, his eyes straying to the longbow and red quiver resting on several pegs pounded into the cabin wall.

Tarwater stopped in the middle of a sentence. His eyes darted from Sadar to the weapon. All the tension, all the restlessness was back on his face. He walked quickly across the room, shook the coffee pot on the stove, and stood indecisively

That fouled the deal for sure, Sadar thought. *I wonder if Tarwater is the one who whipped that arrow at me?*

Standing by the lathe, Sadar decided to tell his story. At first, he fumbled for words, but, after a while, he found them coming easier. As he went on, he realized that never before had he completely unburdened himself of the many details concerned with the lie that had galled him all his life. He told Tarwater about his mother, her loneliness and isolation, of his boyhood fights when other youngsters said he was a thief sprung from a family of thieves. He told how, in junior high school, he had been elected treasurer of some petty organization, and of the humiliation he had felt when, afterward, he had heard one teacher remark to another—"Those kids that elected Sadar were good politicians but poor historians." How both teachers had laughed. And how he had walked into the room and hit one of the teachers in the stomach. He explained what it had been like to be expelled and then made to apologize before the entire school in order to gain reinstatement. That he had made his apology with reservations outlined tersely and privately to the teacher he'd struck, Sadar did not feel necessary to tell Tarwater. He explained simply and without bitterness how his whole life had been colored by a lie and that he wanted to end forever sniping embarrassment.

"I want to live ahead and meet things as they come, without dragging along the curse of something that happened before I was born."

Tarwater had been fumbling absently with the coffee pot when Sadar had started. During the narration he had picked the utensil up and set it down aimlessly several times. Now he was quiet as he looked across the room at Sadar.

"You told me it was better to forget the whole thing," Sadar said, looking Tarwater straight in the eyes. "But you see it can't be done, in my case. You should know that."

"I do know." The deep grooves in Tarwater's cheeks looked like carved marks in dark cedar. His eyes were blank to the present, full of things in the far past. After a full two minutes of moody introspection, he said: "I know what you mean. Things came from the robbery that have sent me out walking in the snow in the middle of the night when I couldn't sleep for thinking. You'd think time would kill things like that. It does in a way, but still there's other times, when things come back so strong the back of your neck feels numb, and you think your head will bust from thinking."

"Those things will never come again. They can't be helped now," Sadar said. "But I have a whole lifetime ahead of me that I can make better by finding the calaverite."

Tarwater stared at him. "It *would* be better for you and Sam if it was found, but God only knows where it is."

"Somebody thinks he does. Somebody tried to kill me since I came to Sylvanite." Sadar kept his eyes off the bow and quiver.

Tarwater did not glance toward them, either. "Kill you? God! I thought all the killing was in the past!" His face became strained; his eyes stared fearfully past Sadar as old memories burned and writhed.

"If you know anything . . . if you have a guess, help me out, Sim."

"Help you . . . ?" Tarwater was a long time coming back to the present, another long time coming to a decision. When he started to speak, he seemed to be talking to someone in years gone by. "I said . . . 'Sam, those shots got me worried.' Mark Besse talked us both out of it. They wasn't right, neither, but then it was too late, and, when I seen Mell's timber station, I was headed to tell Sam. He was fired before I seen him, and I was, too, only I didn't know it. . . . That wasn't right at all." Wonder at an injustice the years hadn't helped him understand was present in Tarwater's soft voice, and he stared at Sadar without seeing him.

"I'm only guessing now, and, even if I'm right, you'd have maybe ninety days of dead work to find out, even if the timber's still holding. If it's gone . . ." Tarwater stopped for several moments as though he were weighing the idea. "I'll tell you what I guessed."

Unconsciously Sadar stepped closer to hear that soft voice.

"Long before the vug was robbed an Injun went into the Big Stope. The damnedest geezer you ever seen, that was. Everybody figured. . . ."

Someone shouted from outside. Little Sim Tarwater jerked nervously, his eyes going toward the bow and arrow on the wall, and then toward the windows that faced the trail outside.

Sadar cursed under his breath, then quickly got control of himself. "What about the Indian?" he urged. "I don't understand."

Another shout came. This time Sadar recognized Jackie's voice. By shifting, he saw her and her father on horses through the barred window. "Let 'em yell a while," he said, but Tarwater was already at the door, and opening it.

"We're just riding by," Jackie called. "Dad's going up to look around the ranch. We thought we'd say hello."

She declined Tarwater's invitation to come inside, commenting that being outdoors "cleared the head of last night's cobwebs."

Sadar stepped over to the lathe. He told himself he wasn't exactly hiding, yet he had no desire to inject his presence into a conversation that might delay the riders from going on about their business, leaving him alone with Tarwater to complete his theory on the missing calaverite. *Indian in the Big Stope . . . Mell's timber station . . . ?* The Indian business didn't make sense, and what this timber station of Mell's was would have to be explained a great deal more.

Returning his gaze to the outside, he watched the morning sunlight shimmer across Jackie's hair as she moved her head. Rouvière sat his horse solidly, his blunt face unreadable. Something about Rouvière gave the man an air of ruthless vigilance wherever one encountered him.

He heard Jackie laugh and warn Tarwater against letting Chinook inside the cabin. Rouvière inquired whether Tarwater had seen any cattle stray up the river from his ranch. Tarwater hadn't seen any lately, he said. "Some catch 'em, some don't," he told Rouvière in reply to a question about the fishing.

Presently the riders went on. Tarwater shut the door quietly.

All the fever was back in Tarwater's eyes. He moved restlessly as though memories were thrusting knives in him again. "She worries about me and Chinook," he muttered. He looked out the windows, then glanced around the room nervously. "I've got to do something," he said.

"What you told me isn't clear," Sadar said.

"Not clear," Tarwater repeated. "Well, it was just a guess, young Sam . . . just a bad guess, maybe."

He went across the room and got his bow and quiver. He started for the door.

For an instant Sadar considered stopping him by force, but saner thinking brushed the thought away instantly.

"I'll go with you," Sadar said.

"No!" Tarwater paused at the door. "I may be gone all day. Make yourself to home."

The door closed without a sound, and Sadar saw the little archer go past the window above the stove. He sat down in the rawhide chair, vowing to himself that he would not leave the cabin until Tarwater had returned and made clear his cloudy statements. No use to curse the luck that had sent Rouvière and Jackie riding by at the wrong time. Was it luck? They were on the mountain quite early. Whatever the reason, something about their presence had upset Tarwater tremendously.

Sadar got up and began to pace the room. Ninety days of dead work, Tarwater had said, even if his guess was right. Ninety days of mucking, timbering, catching up ground that might be loose for hundreds of vertical feet, only to get to some place that had been searched forty-five years before, a place where Sim *guessed* the calaverite might be.

According to Ben, Tarwater hadn't set foot in a mine for almost a half century, yet he had been able to make an estimate of the time necessary to clear a way. Tarwater's estimate was probably based on conditions forty-five years before. The same question kept rumbling through Sadar's mind: *How had the thieves reached the place?*

Ninety days or ninety months, the job had to be done someday. The fluorspar deal was about a dead duck by now, anyway. As Sadar walked the floor, he knew he was going to stay in Sylvanite and keep trying as long as there was a chance to find twenty-seven ancient sacks of high grade.

Another pact with himself having been made, he broke the one he had made a few moments earlier—that of staying until Tarwater came back. Tarwater could be gone all day and half the night, sleeping in a cave somewhere with his head pillowed on that damned mountain lion.

Chapter Twelve

CAVE-IN

The live hole at which Sadar stopped lay athwart the ski course on top of Sylvan Mountain. Rock ledges on both sides showed why Rouvière could not have moved the extension out of this saddle without great expense. The two old men had been mighty sharp in staking this fraction.

A tiny blacksmith's shop with a forge stack made of carbide cans sat on the edge of the trees. No one was around. If fresh muck on the dump and the location of the shaft hadn't already convinced him, Sadar would have known Ducray had a hand in the mine when he discovered the precisely framed cribbing. He stood with one hand resting on the windlass beam for a moment, then lowered himself into the man-way and climbed down.

The shaft ended on a dry bottom. Using matches, he explored a narrow drift approximately thirty feet long, ending up against a freshly shot breast where a half-inch streak of sylvanite wandered through the gangue. He lit several matches at once to examine the pay streak. A half inch wasn't much, and sylvanite was notorious for pinching to nothing without warning, but still it was plenty while it lasted. A wise miner would stay with that streak even if it left the shaft, went over the dump, and climbed a yellow pine tree. In single jack mining the streak would pay its way.

He was halfway out of the shaft when a shadow fell across the collar. He looked up to see Ben and Ducray framed against the sky.

Ben's big voice boomed down at him. "Shall we drop rocks on him now, Deedee . . . or shoot him for a high-grader when he gets out?"

Sadar laughed. "Hold your fire, boys! I surrender."

"Let's make him work on the windlass all day," Ducray suggested.

Sadar climbed on out.

The two old men were in digging clothes and were carrying lunch buckets. There was no denying the competent hard-bodied look of Ben Liggett, but still Sadar was disturbed by the impression that Ben was out of place in rough, working garb. He attributed the feeling to the fact that the first time he'd seen Ben, the old man was standing behind a bar in a white shirt.

"You get around early," Ducray said.

"I've been around to see Sim already."

Ben stared down the shaft. "What do you think of our hole?"

"You got a nice streak down there . . . I'd like to have twenty-seven sacks of that stuff."

Ducray laughed. "So would we." His lively brown eyes drooped at the outer corners and twinkled at Sadar. "You weren't looking for calaverite, by any chance?"

"Your workings are too new. I got to prowl some of the old ones to do that."

"Better stay clear of the Hibernian," Ducray warned. "Ralston is touchy as hell about those holes, and he . . . well, he can't help his temper some of the time. I haven't been in the Hibe for years, but I can pretty well tell you what you'll find in the Vivandière. I went through all the open levels with Rouvière last year, when he was sort of figuring on opening some of it up."

"What will I find?"

"Cave-ins," Ben said gloomily.

Sadar considered this information. After all, in spite of his determination not to waste time looking at the same ground hundreds had searched in vain, he didn't have anything else to do. He could take a look around the Vivandière for a few hours, then go back and try to catch Tarwater at home. "How many holes can I get into?" he asked Ducray.

Ducray pushed out his lips and thought. "Zero's in from the surface. One was open last year for six, seven hundred feet of the main drift . . . on Two the whole country is down from the. . . ."

"How about showing me around?" Sadar asked. Suddenly he remembered the two weeks' wages from Rouvière. He took the money out of his pocket and explained its source, omitting Reeves's duplicity in the hiring, although he suspected Ben and Ducray guessed the truth about that. He held the money toward Ben. "I'm not trying to buy anything with it. It's just that I feel the same way you fellows do about Reeves and his ideas. Take it and buy a bottle or two of whisky for the back-bar."

He had expected the most opposition from Ducray, but he didn't seem to be thinking about the money. He had an absent-minded, wistful look on his face. Ben's eyes were hard and expressionless.

"Damn it! It isn't charity!" Sadar pronounced. "Are you going to take it or not?"

Ben's brown face spread in a slow grin. "Sure, we'll take it. Thanks."

"He gets sore at himself just like Grandpa Sam when he

was trying to help someone out," Ducray said quietly, addressing Ben.

"You knew my grandfather pretty well?"

"He was a shifter at the Digman long before he ever went to the Viv as superintendent," Ducray explained. "Sam's the one who got me loose and carried me out of a bad stope the time I got this hip, when everyone else had run like hell." His eyes went vague, and he stared at the town far below. "Many's the time I played poker with Sam Rigdon."

Ben, too, seemed saddened by thoughts of days that would not come again. He stared moodily at the blacksmith's shop.

Sadar was embarrassed. "Speaking of poker, what kind of millionaire's game is that bunch with Jammer playing at the Fire Horse?"

"Millionaire's game?" Ducray said blankly. He and Ben stared at each other.

"I tried to donate that money I just gave you, and Jammer offered me three white chips. Not a damned soul cracked a smile, either!"

Ben leaned on the windlass upright and began to laugh like a foghorn gone wild. Ducray's shoulders shook, and he closed his eyes and showed his teeth and gasped with laughter until Sadar thought the old man would choke.

"He jobbed you!" Ben groaned. "There ain't a cent in that game!" He began to laugh again.

Ducray nodded, his face red from laughing. "He's hell for a joke. Jammer's face has fooled older men than you. Of course, the crowd went along with him!"

Sadar grinned. "I wasn't sure, but I'll admit they made me turn tail like a pup that had wandered into a dog fight."

Five minutes later, carrying freshly filled lamps, Sadar followed Ducray along the top of the mountain.

"What makes Ralston so sure the calaverite is in the Hibernian?" Sadar asked. "Well, there's no question but what the vug was robbed from the Hibe stope, and I guess it's as good a place as any to figure."

They walked on through the trees.

"Did you ever hear of an Indian in the Big Stope, a funny sort of geezer?" Sadar asked.

Ducray's brown eyes went wide. "A geezer of an Indian?" He thought a moment. "You mean the one in the lobby, the one that used to be by the cigar stand?"

"Wrong Indian."

Ducray glared at him in exasperation.

As Ducray had said, Zero Vivandière, at the very top of the hill, was down like a glory hole. Rotting ends of posts showed above cave workings.

"Closer to a quarry than a mine," Ducray commented.

They went down the mountain to Number One. Standing at the concreted portal, Ducray adjusted his lamp and lit it. "I guess you know everybody in the country has been through these holes at one time or another, looking for those sacks of high grade."

Sadar nodded. "Let's go in."

Damp coolness in the old bore wrapped itself around them. The rectangle of light behind them grew smaller and smaller. Their feet sent thumping concussions deeper and deeper into the dark. Small sloughs from the solid bore had trapped small pools of water. They slopped through and went on. No raises, no cross-cuts—nothing diverged from the transit-straight line of the tunnel. Hissing flames from the lamps made their shadows jerk unevenly on the cold walls. Ducray's voice rang hollowly when he stated what Sadar already had guessed.

"This was drove to get under the original discovery at Zero."

They came against a solid block of caved rocks. Ducray raised his lamp. "This is the end. We're under Zero, and the whole country is down from here to the surface."

They went toward the sunlight, sloshing through icy pools.

Sadar counted three hundred steps from the portal of Two before they were blocked off by an oozing muck pile. He stepped forward and examined the choke of slime, thick pink mud, small rocks, and broken timber. "We must be somewhere close to being dead under that place where the railroad goes across an old stope."

Ducray swung his lamp upward as though he could follow its light to the surface. "Yup, almost dead under. Forty, fifty feet ahead of us is a stope that runs clear to the surface from this level and down to about fifty feet above the level below us."

"Then this drift doesn't go beyond the stope?" Sadar asked.

"Hell, yes! It runs, or used to run, a mile or more farther into the hill."

"Must have been some timbering job to carry this track where it goes through the stope," Sadar said.

"I never did see it, but men that did told me this level was just a long, flat box, bulkheaded top and bottom. The stulls were Oregon fir, fifty feet long. Miners that worked in there told me, when they'd run a string of cars fast along that bulkhead, it sounded like being inside a bull-hide drum surrounded with thunder."

Sadar's light glistened on the water dripping from the roof. He looked more closely at the oozing muck pile. Somewhere not too far beyond that plug of débris was a body of water reaching up toward the surface, lying black and cold far back into the long drift. He felt a sudden urge to leave the place fast, thinking of the dismal *ca-choom!* sound the rock had made when he tossed it into the depths from the old railroad grade.

"That's the place where I told you the engine dropped," Ducray said. "It tore hell out of the bulkhead and went clear to the bottom of the stope . . . and there she is today, if she ain't rusted to nothing." The old man started easing backward. "I wouldn't want to be in front of that muck, if it started slipping. Let's sort of get out of here."

Outside, they shut off their lamps and let the sunshine soak into their bodies. "Want to look at some more of them?" Ducray asked.

Sadar scraped his mud-laden shoe against a rusty rail. "May as well." As they started down the hill, he said: "Ever hear of a man named Mell?"

Ducray gave him a quick glance. "Jason Mell, you mean? Why he was one of the Vivandière men killed during the trouble after the vug was robbed. Where'd you ever hear of him?"

"Ran across his name in some old files at the *Times*," Sadar lied. "Was he a Hibernian miner?"

"No, he worked at the Vivandière. Timberman or trammer, I forget which." Ducray laughed. "I remember him best by the way he used to get drunk and tear hell out of some of the old parlor houses."

So Mell had been killed after the robbery. *Mell's timber station.* Must have been in the Vivandière, all right. Maybe Mell had been involved in the robbery along with several Hibernian men. The sacks could have gone from that abandoned Hibernian stope by some little used combination of workings back into the Vivandière. Yes, maybe back into the

Vivandière—or into some other mine a quarter of a mile away. Just how far those sacks had gone from the vug after removal depended on how much time there had been on that night forty-five years ago. For the first time Sadar fully appreciated how cold the trail was that he was trying to follow.

They turned on the lanterns, and went into Number Three.

A thousand feet of tunnel and endless shallow pools trapped by small sloughs lay between them and the portal when they passed a sagging chute and the dark blot of a raise that held the first stick of timber they had encountered on this level. They went approximately two hundred feet farther and were stopped by a jam of oozy muck laced with a jackstraw tangle of soggy timbers.

Ducray swung his light across the face of the cave-in. Water was working from the muck, curling a slow flow around the ends of timber that rested against a long pile spiling that angled across the drift. Sadar tapped the spiling with the side of his fist. It was drum-tight at the lower end, but didn't look very securely held in the niche where pressure had forced its lower end. He knew that time had robbed the timber of its strength, but he remembered the old miner's saw that no timber could hold ground—timber merely kept ground from getting started. Although there was little life in that piece of spiling, it could very well be holding the entire jam.

"I wouldn't want the contract to clear this mess," Sadar said.

"It's that, sure enough," Ducray agreed. "This comes from the old raise that led up to the bottom of the stope about fifty feet above us, up there where the locomotive is. If you thought there was a lot of water piled above us when we were up on the next level, think of the mess of it overhead now."

Sadar didn't like what his imagination pictured. Nor did he like the oozing muck pile and the haphazardly wedged piece of spiling that seemed to be holding everything back. He rubbed his foot in slime that was as slick as mossy rocks in the bottom of a stream, and held his lamp steady on the jam to kill the impression that the whole block was moving.

"Let's get out of here," Ducray suggested.

"Suits me."

As Ducray turned, he slipped. With his free hand Sadar grabbed the old man's arm. Ducray's right arm went back to catch something. His lamp *clunked* soggily into the piece of angled spiling, and then his shoulder struck against the upper end of the timber. He stumbled for balance, gained it, and cursed. "No wonder I'm always hurting my hip!"

Sadar looked at the piece of spiling. Ducray's shoulder had knocked it loose at the upper end, and now the pole lay across the muck pile. Sadar steadied his light, cursing the shadows that gave the jam a moving appearance. The hackles on his spine rose, and his back tingled. The muck pile *was* moving. It was coming slowly toward them, the ends of broken timber twisting a little.

Ducray saw it, too. "Hellfire and little fishes!" he cried hoarsely. "Let's go!"

They stumbled and slipped on the slimy ties and rails, throwing their hands against the sides of the bore to keep from falling. Ducray jammed his burner into the wall, and the lamp went dead. He dropped it with a hoarse oath. "Get ahead, so I can see!" he yelled.

Sadar was already moving past him. As he ran, he tried to think. They were a long distance in, but the muck might be slow in breaking loose, or might even choke up again. But if it moved far enough to let the water behind it get started. . . . He thought of the raise they'd passed. They could take a chance on that . . . if there was a ladder left or enough sound timber to hold a man's weight. . . . He started to shout his thoughts to Ducray as they neared the raise.

Then behind them sounded a thump that caused the light to flicker and whistle. They heard a sucking noise as if the mountain had drawn a deep breath through a lake of thick mud. For an instant they heard nothing but the pounding of their own footsteps. They ran past the raise.

Ducray's hand slapped hard against Sadar's heel, almost tripping him. "My hip!" he grunted.

He was flat on the tunnel floor when Sadar turned and came back.

"Get to hell out!" Ducray shouted. "Go on!"

Ground groaned and shifted. Timber broke with a strangely muffled crack, and they heard another, louder, heavier *thump*.

Ducray rolled and sat up. "Get out!" he ordered.

Sadar thrust the light at the old man. He picked Ducray up and staggered deeper into the mountain, straight back toward the awesome rumbling sounds. The eight or nine steps he took to reach the raise seemed the longest distance he had ever walked.

He lifted Ducray as high as he could toward the man-way. "Grab something," he shouted.

Holding the lamp, Ducray strained to reach overhead. Some of his weight went from Sadar. Damp wood broke with a pulpy sound. All Ducray's weight came back on Sadar. Both men nearly fell. Sadar staggered and shifted his grip until he had Ducray midway between knee and thigh. He made another lift, slipping sideways in the slime underfoot.

"For God's sake, grab something!"

They heard the tunnel give out a long, gushing sigh. The sounds of water thundered in the bore.

All Ducray's weight left Sadar. He looked up to see the old man scrambling toward a gap in the partition between chute and man-way. The lamp was hanging on a ladder rung above the first one that had broken under Ducray's weight. As he leaped to catch the rung, Sadar knew it was too high. He fell back, expecting to feel the smash of mud and timber against his legs.

The tunnel was filled with the sullen bellow of oncoming mud and débris.

"Grab my hands!" Ducray was draped on his belly across the partition, reaching down with both muddy hands.

Sadar leaped again, grabbing with his left hand for the side of the ladder at the broken rung. His other hand went past Ducray's extended fingers, but the old man's grip clamped onto Sadar's wrist. They were both helpless for a moment, Ducray's face twisted, and his teeth showing.

Something jarred hard against Sadar. One leg went numb. Somehow, slowly, with one foot against the sloping wall, his left hand breaking fingernails on damp wood, and Ducray pulling on his right wrist, Sadar drew himself up to the partition.

Something like a sob came from Ducray, and he hung so limply for a moment that Sadar thought he was unconscious from the pain. He grabbed by the X of Ducray's overalls.

"I won't fall, Sam," Ducray muttered.

The tunnel began to roar as if a hundred midget racers were speeding down it. Air rising from the dark flood caused the lamp flame to gutter upward and whine shrilly. Above them long sheets of white mold hung from damp timber like trailing remnants of fouled sails in the tangled rigging of a sunken ship. The rising air didn't reach high in the dead pocket of the raise, but it came high enough to make the lamp protest, to stir the ends of the ghostly drapes of mold. With it came the odors of rotting timber, foul mud, damp rock, and the faint smell of powder gas that seems to cling forever to blasted rock underground.

Below them the chute gates, posts, and the bottom of the chute were carried away and smashed almost before going out of sight. Timber flung sideways across the bore broke apart. Other timbers were borne against the side of the raise and shot upward as if trying to claw their way out of the rushing flood.

They went higher in the man-way as the water rose, sending slaps of mud upward. Spread like frogs to place their weight as close as possible to the junction of the rungs with the two-by-fours that formed the sides of the ladder, they wiped the clinging sheets of mold from their faces by brushing them against their shoulders, and hung on, breathing dead air and praying that the rungs would hold.

The water was moving so fast now it appeared to be motionless, although it flared angrily against timbers that tried to lodge across the bore. At times the mountain groaned from the shift of the terrible weight. In these moments they could feel faint vibrations in the solid rock.

Above them the shroud-like drapes hung motionless. Below them the water pounded until its loudness reduced itself in their ears to a humming constancy. Their heads began to ache from the dead air. Sweat soaked their bodies; their feet felt numbed from their wet shoes.

Ducray kept shifting gently on the ladder above Sadar in an effort to take weight from his game hip. He spoke only once after climbing higher in the raise. "It twists my guts to even think of it," he said.

Chapter Thirteen

AFTER THE FLOOD

For three hours the flood roared past. Sometimes it slackened, but would then come back with a bellow when débris, only momentarily blocked, broke loose with tremendous thumps.

Quiet fell so quickly their ears seemed plugged. The flood was there one moment. The next the tunnel was still, except for the dripping of water from the roof. Tommy-knockers rapped somewhere in the workings. Ground shifted and gave forth an unearthly groan. They waited a half hour longer to be sure.

Holding his breath, Sadar dropped from the man-way to the tunnel floor, and then helped down Ducray. Their light was almost dead. Both were limping as they set off down the bore toward the sunlight. No rail, no tie, no scrap of timber, or loose piece of rock as large as a man's hand remained in the tunnel. The flood had left only a thin film of pink mud.

"It's a good thing you fell," Sadar said. "We never would have made it out."

Ducray nodded. His face was gray where it wasn't muddy.

They reached the portal, and, after the darkness of the tunnel, the harsh light made them squint their eyes. Once his eyes had adjusted to the outside world, Sadar looked around. It seemed to Sadar that everybody in Sylvanite was on the dump, or the half of the dump that was left. The others were spread in a wide pink fan at the edge of town on the end of a channel cut to bedrock all the way down the mountain. Green fragments of mangled trees showed in the wash. The old caved stope near the base of the hill was a lake of bobbing cans and trash boxes. Two boys on a plank raft were exploring it. The big mine building on the dump had been sliced away to the boiler foundation.

The crowd looked at the two muddy men as if they were ghosts. Then everyone began to shout at once, rushing toward Sadar and Ducray.

Overwhelmed, Ducray sat down. "This is worse than the flood," he said.

Quick-striding Rouvière and Ben Liggett headed toward the two survivors, side by side. Behind them, Sadar saw Reeves and Jackie, the red-bearded man shouldering people aside with insolent carelessness as he held the girl's arm and maneuvered her through the crush. Standing above the portal like a lean, sneering wolf was Jack Ralston.

Ben's deep shout brought momentary quiet. He raised thick brown-mottled arms and rumbled: "Let 'em talk!"

The roar of the crowd quieted as suddenly as had the flood in the tunnel. Hundreds of eyes settled on Sadar, who was standing.

"We walked inside, saw water pushing a cave-in toward us, went up a raise, and let her run," Sadar summed up their adventure.

Ben's slate eyes smiled briefly. Some of the crowd laughed, and others howled for details. Rouvière's face showed that he was not even mildly amused.

"That's all there was to it," Ducray affirmed. "There must have been some water in there some place."

Somewhere in the crowd Sadar heard Myra giggle.

Rouvière's voice was crisp. "What were you doing on my property in the first place?"

"Looking for Easter eggs, P.T.F.!" a gangly youth in a T-shirt yelled.

The crowd laughed.

Rouvière didn't seem to hear. His eyes shifted from Sadar to Ducray. The hammer-like flatness of his jaw and mouth barely moved when he stated: "You caused a lot of damage."

"*We* caused it!" Sadar stared at the millionaire. "Do you think we cut loose a body of stale water like that deliberately?"

"You were in there when it happened!" Rouvière snapped.

"Sure they did it, P.T.F.!" the skinny youth yelled. "They left the bathtub running!"

This, the response of the crowd seemed to say, was going to be a pretty good show.

Jackie pushed past Rouvière and Ben. She placed a hand on Ben's shoulder, and Sadar could see she was trembling. "Instead of this public forum to establish a case of guilt," she said, looking directly into her father's eyes, "suppose we get Deedee off the hill. He looks like he could stand a ride."

"These two men deliberately . . . ," Rouvière began.

"Yes, Dad, yes! You can sue them later." She looked at Reeves. "How about bringing my horse over here, Biff?"

"Get the goil's charger, bum!" the skinny heckler shouted.

Jackie smothered a smile, and, turning her gaze toward Sadar, said: "You certainly know how to draw a crowd."

"Looks like we got everybody out but Terry and Gary," Sadar said.

"Who,"—Jackie pointed toward the pink lake below Number Six Vivandière—"do you think is out on that raft down there?"

Rouvière was already riding down the mountain, sun glinting on his bald head, when Ben and Sadar helped Ducray onto the horse. Myra, Jackie, and Reeves left with Ben and Ducray. Above the concreted portal Ralston kept his position aloof from the crowd, watching like a malign figurehead.

It wasn't long before those from the crowd that had remained behind began to press hard around Sadar, asking questions. His bruised leg was beginning to hurt, so he hobbled over toward the portal and sat down on the slope of the hill. A large part of the crowd moved right along with him, some arguing about the amount of water that had gushed from the tunnel, some declaring that there probably was twice that much left inside. A few curious onlookers ventured a short distance into the tunnel, led by the gangly heckler, who had collected a rather substantial following of teenagers.

Suddenly the youth came charging from the bore, bellowing that he heard more water coming. Those at the portal scattered. A red-faced fat man wearing fishing boots was knocked down, scrambled to his feet, and was knocked down again. The crowd rocked with laughter.

Old Charley, appearing suddenly out of the remaining throng, thumped Sadar's shoulder and cackled. "You sure pried up hell that trip, young Sam!"

Before responding, Sadar began taking his lamp apart. Then: "Those stopes must have been regular lakes with underground fish, Charley." He dumped the expended carbide on the ground, almost on the feet of two girls wearing Western costumes. One of the girls sported a long streamer across her front. **Boom Days Queen**, it announced. She wrinkled her nose at the rank carbide odor and said: "*Phew!*"

"No likum smellum, Queenie?" the kid in the T-shirt asked.

"That's just one stope in there . . . not two," Charley said.

"You ought to know, Charley!" the teenager continued to jibe. "You thought the railroad ran through there once!"

When he could be heard, Sadar asked Charley: "Did *you* drop that engine?"

"I'm the one!" Charley said proudly. "A light Six-Hundred she was . . . then right smack into that stope above Number Two, one day, when I was coming down from the Evening Star." He glanced at Sadar. "Didn't you know that?"

"I didn't know you were the engineer."

"I mean I was!" Old Charley looked around at the crowd. "I'd helped Ben Liggett up the hill with a string of ore cars. . . ." Charley had some difficulty recalling who Ben's foreman had been. He got into a sharp argument over the man's name with another old-timer. He described the weather, cursed a track crew who didn't know how to clean a crossing properly, and extolled the beauty of a waitress at the Evening Star boarding house. At last he got started down the hill, digressing to explain that the air brakes on the Old 607, as she was known, were not up to snuff, because shop men always did more damage than good when they worked on a locomotive. If you wanted things fixed right, you always had to stop on the road somewhere and do the job yourself.

Eventually Charley put Old 607 into the stope. "The fireman had unloaded. I'd opened my water brake valve and rared back on the Johnson bar, but she was still rolling toward that sagged place in the rails. So I left her. When the pony trucks hit that cracked place . . . how the hell we didn't fall in on the way up is beyond me . . . the ingine just tip-ended and went down like that!" He slid one hand down the back of the other. "The last I seen is the back of the tender . . . the next minute the mountain sounds like it's rolling its guts!"

"Anybody working down below?" Sadar asked.

"Nope!" Charley stated. "That stope was cleaned out and bulkheaded off years before. My Six Hundred tore out a pile of bulkheads on Two level, but they started timbering her up before the steam cleared out . . . and, believe me, that mine was full of steam!"

Charley went into a description of the locomotive as he'd seen it in the bottom of the stope, but Sadar wasn't listening. He was struggling to recapture a thought that had come to the front of his mind, then darted back, just as a familiar name can elude one right when he thinks he has it.

"When *was* that?" Sadar asked.

"Oh, Eighteen . . . no, Nineteen . . . dag-goned if I can say exact. It was before I was married, the first time." Charley tilted his head and thought. The teenager asked if it was the winter of '76, and Charley told him to go to hell. "It was about two years before the vug was robbed!" Charley finally announced.

Two years before the robbery. Sadar wondered how well that stope had been sealed up after the engine tore things up. Surely it must have been searched, but, even if it hadn't, the problem of getting to it now would be enormous.

Terry and Gary were still on their raft, visibly experimenting to see how far they could rock the raft without spilling themselves into the water, when Sadar set off by himself down the mountain. He hadn't gone far when Ralston overtook him.

"Nice deal you pulled up there," he said.

Sadar held his temper. "Yup! Every Wednesday Deedee and I try to drown ourselves some way."

"Very unfunny!"

"That depends on whether or not you got a mind like a stack of old battery plates eaten up with acid." Sadar glanced at Ralston's hip pocket. The automatic was still there.

"It'll cost you more than a suit for damages, if you monkey with the Hibernian," Ralston warned.

"Such as what?"

"Don't be starting any floods on my property. Just don't even fool around it!"

"Don't blow your top, Ralston, until you catch me moving a rock on one of your lousy dumps."

Ralston's look was bubbling with vicious anger. His face grew lumpy and dark. For a moment Sadar thought the man's temper would lead him to violence. But Ralston took it out in a venomous stare and walked on ahead. "Remember what I told you," he called back.

Sadar limped on down the trail, telling himself that he had a lot of things to find out. He began to regret that he had angered Ralston. That bitter, narrow-shouldered man might have a good lead on the calaverite, after all. Sadar had one dangerous enemy already, assuming that Ralston was *not* the one who had loosed the arrow and pushed in the rocks at the old Commander portal.

He wondered again about the stope where Charley's Six Hundred had plunged. Surely every possible hiding place in the Vivandière or any adjacent mine had been scoured by men who knew the workings well. Maybe the ore had been distributed behind side lagging; maybe the sacks, ore and all, had been dropped into some abandoned winze full of water. He didn't like that last thought at all. There had been twenty-seven sacks of high grade and limited time to carry them to concealment. He had to believe time had been short, or else accept the certainty that the ore had been taken completely out of the mountain. The number of sacks and the time involved seemed to prove that several miners had worked together in the theft, perhaps the very five that Ben said had been killed afterward. After all, one man might have had the patience to try a plan that meant years of waiting, but not several men.

Between the information Rouvière must possess and what Tarwater had guessed, a man might be able to work out a pretty sound theory—if he could get all the facts from both of them. *Injun went into the Big Stope . . . damnedest geezer. . . .* The thought flashed through Sadar's mind that Reeves should hire Tarwater to write the clues for his treasure hunt.

When he reached Sylvanite, he went directly to the Fire Horse. Ben Liggett hadn't changed clothes, and Sadar found him sitting at the long table in the barroom, his big brown-mottled hands clasped on the wood before him.

"Deedee all right?" Sadar asked.

Ben raised heavy brows. "He got in and out of that outdoor shower of his. Any man that can do that is healthy."

Sadar sat down on the table corner. "What did you warn me about, Ben?"

Ben's slate eyes regarded Sadar gloomily. "I said I might have been wrong. I still say it. Maybe I was only guessing."

"Who did you warn me about?"

Ben shook his big head slowly.

"Did you know a Vivandière miner named Jason Mell?"

"Jason Mell . . . God! That's a long time ago. Funny thing about Jason. 'Most everybody blamed the operators for killing him, but there was a story that Mell and a trammer from the Viv was killed by the Hibe miners who robbed the vug . . . before they got knocked over themselves. If you can make any sense out of that, you're welcome to it."

"What about a geezer of an Indian at the Big Stope?"

Ben gave him a blank look. "There was this wooden Indian there years ago. What are you trying to get at?"

"I'll be damned if I know," Sadar said in disgust.

"Where'd you get the Indian business?"

"Sim. He told me a few things that mixed me up more than ever."

Ben nodded. "Sim's like that when he gets to talking fast. His words get all twisted when he thinks of those toughs blowed up in the barracks at night. It's enough to give any man bad thoughts."

Sadar glanced at the ancient photos on the wall, feeling the impact of the past in them and Ben's heavy manner. He knew he'd been stirring up bad memories, exposing old hurts ever since he'd been in Sylvanite. But he had to jab and probe—or else make poor guesses. He studied Ben's broad face for a long time.

"Who was on the other detonator box . . . the one that did the job?" Sadar asked.

Ben's slate eyes were inscrutable. "Me."

Silence ran as dead as when a man stands in a mine until his ears hear sounds that are not there. That he had been the agent to make old ghosts writhe and show their teeth Sadar could not deny. That it had to be so he regretted.

Suddenly he realized he had heard no noise from the casino. That poker game was just another of the fragments that fitted nowhere, yet helped tangle his thinking. He asked about the Swede.

"Jammer's got a little ranch down the river. I think the whole gang is down there fishing today. Winters, he goes to Arizona or some place where it's warm."

"For a high-country ranch income, that isn't bad."

Ben made slow card-dealing motions. "Slickers see that dumb face and beg him to get in . . . the first time."

Sadar began to see bright light about Jammer Roos and the odd poker game, but it wasn't light that led toward twenty-seven sacks of calaverite resting in the dark of Sylvan Mountain.

He left the long room with its dark furniture and the photographs and the heavy figure sitting at the table. Ben's eyes were on his hands, and his face was solemn with hindsight of ancient things as Sadar closed the door.

His fourth day was almost gone. The thought didn't trouble him as much as it would have two days before.

Chapter Fourteen

A BIG DEAL

Back at the Big Stope, Sadar showered and changed clothes, having decided to follow the Indian lead, fantastic as it seemed.

After dinner he found Jackie Rouvière and Myra lolling in the red jeep just beyond the brightest area of light thrown by the carbide lamps under the marquee.

Myra grinned at him impudently. "We were just a little late today, but we promise to be on time next time you need saving."

Sadar grinned. "You did well enough the first time."

He looked at Jackie. There was a marked resemblance between her eyes and Rouvière's, but the exact way of describing it was hard to fix.

"What's wrong with my face?" Myra asked.

"I've been looking at for years now, every time I find myself in a post office studying the posters," Sadar told her with a grin.

"He's doing better, Jackie," Myra said critically. "The night he got his beard yanked, all he could do was ogle like a trout watching a minnow he couldn't get." She offered Sadar a cigarette. "Naturally you don't know that Jackie talked her old man out of suing the pants off you and Deedee for malicious destruction of property, endangering lives, washing out bridle paths, spoiling natural beauty. . . ."

"Myra, you're a stool pigeon!" Jackie inserted into her friend's litany.

"If the light was good, you could see a rosy blush," Myra insisted, picking up a new topic with which to run. Sadar wondered if she might be related to Mrs. Mahogany. "Of course, you know Jackie did it all for Deedee. You just happened to fall under her protective mantle." She sighed lugubriously. "I wish I could lure somebody into my powerhouse so gently. I'd consider little Sim Tarwater . . . if I can only get him away from that lion for a few minutes."

Jackie laughed. "Myra's mother was marked by a phonograph! Pay no attention."

"What a perfectly Victorian idea!" Myra giggled. "Biff can have Pete Dill use it in his advertising."

"Speaking of Sim Tarwater," Sadar said to Jackie, "did you know you and your dad scared him into the woods right in the middle of an important conversation with me?"

He couldn't be sure of Jackie's expression, even though he leaned toward her a little.

"I didn't know we scared him off, but Dad knew you were in the cabin. He saw you strike up the hill early in the morning when he was getting up. Of course, your fresh tracks in the dew didn't hurt any, either."

"Sim grabbed his bow and arrows and ran," Sadar said.

"Don't let that throw you off," Jackie said. "Sim carries that bow and his quiver like some men wear a wrist watch."

That might be, Sadar thought, *but he had been without his equipment the night I had met him on the deserted street—unless it had been cached somewhere nearby.*

"While we're in the bow and arrow department, what can you tell me about a geezer of an Indian here in the hotel?" Sadar asked casually.

"I saw a geezer once in Yellowstone," Myra joked.

Jackie's voice held curious tension when she said: "Yes, there's a cigar store Indian around the hotel some place. How could that possibly interest you?"

"He's a squawman," Myra said. "Or is that gilded thing in the basement a buck?"

Sadar said nothing, still watching Jackie's face. She was the only one he had questioned about the Indian subject whose reaction seemed something other than puzzlement. Overall, this encounter was not changing Sadar's opinion about Jackie. She was a strange one. *And what exactly had Myra meant when she had said Jackie protected Deedee?* Sadar wondered.

"Are you looking for calaverite . . . or *what?*" Jackie asked.

"Just calaverite," Sadar said. "I'll see you later."

"He left us for a painted dummy." Sadar heard Myra mourn as he walked toward the hotel.

At the timber rigging, just inside the doorway of the hotel, Sadar met Reeves, who bobbed his red beard curtly and would have passed without a word if Sadar hadn't moved carelessly to block him.

Reeves's eyes tightened at the corners. Reddish glints seemed to leap into them.

"I promise not to keep you long," Sadar assured Reeves. "I've just been wondering what was the rest of that deal you were about to make the other day?"

"Deal?" Reeves affected surprise. "I hired you as a ski instructor. Since then, Mister Rouvière has pointed out my error, and sober reflection has shown me he is right. That is as far as any *deal* went, Sadar. My only interest in you, now, is as a guest of the hotel. If you have any complaints or suggestions, tell the clerk."

"You mentioned the maps of the Vivandière levels," Sadar persisted. "How did they tie up with skiing, Reeves?"

"In the course of the conversation that might have slipped in some way. At any rate, I've locked up the maps since then, and they are not available to unauthorized personnel."

"You read too many signs during the war, I see."

Reeves smiled coldly. He brushed past Sadar and continued out of the hotel. Sadar watched him cross the walk and stop near the jeep. He said something to the girls, then glanced back toward Sadar with a mocking smile.

Sadar hated him more than ever then. Reeves had changed his mind fast enough, all right, but not because of anything Rouvière might have said. It was at the Commander portal that the red-bearded man had come to the conclusion that Sadar didn't know a thing about the calaverite and was prowling aimlessly. That much was sure in Sadar's mind. Not so certain was what Reeves knew.

As he neared the desk, Terry and Gary appeared, hovering about him like flies on a sweating horse. They pestered him with questions and mixed in useless and uninteresting information about their own adventures on the raft until he picked them both up by the pants and threatened to knock their heads together.

"Do it! Go ahead!" one said. "Mine's the hardest."

He put the boys down and grinned at Al. The bellhops scampered for the door, when car lights struck against the windows. One managed to trip the other so that he did a belly slide for ten feet on the waxed linoleum tile.

Al grinned. "I don't know whether I could stand more than two weeks of those outlaws, but you got to admit they're genuine."

"Genuine fools," Sadar agreed while continuing to smile. "Al, can you tell me who put the maps in the office safe the other day?" Sadar asked casually.

Without missing a beat, Al answered: "Rouvière."

Sadar felt mildly pleased with himself for having guessed that Reeves had lied. Being a man constitutionally opposed to having his importance lessened, Reeves had taken credit for Rouvière's move. To Sadar, this act of Rouvière's proved the millionaire didn't trust Reeves concerning the high grade, at least not since Sadar's arrival. But that was all it proved. *I'm nibbling at the edges,* Sadar thought, *but I can't get a solid bite at anything.*

He let his eyes travel around the lobby. Mrs. Mahogany was emerging from the dining room, scanning the horizon for a lover of things Victorian or someone to convert to that condition. Terry and Gary were busy at the street entrance, grunting under the weight of the luggage of a middle-aged couple that looked tired and ready to complain about something in advance. Sadar looked back at Mrs. Mahogany, estimating the prospects of avoiding her if he paused at the desk long enough to ask Al about the Indian. Then he saw something that washed that concern out of his mind. Jack Ralston and Rouvière were just rising from a table in the dining room. *There*, Sadar thought, *is the hatching of a deal I'd like to know about.*

His speculative decision turned out to have cost him dearly, for Mrs. Mahogany had gone into overdrive and was engulfing him with a delighted—"Well! Mister Sadar!"—just as the newcomers arrived at the desk.

Terry and Gary began dropping the couple's bags on each other's feet, as the middle-aged couple edged past them to the desk. Their elbows planted solidly on the front desk, the couple turned in Sadar's direction, sniffing suspiciously as though they had detected the smell of cooking cauliflower. Mrs. Mahogany took the opportunity to steer Sadar toward several chairs parked adjacent to a nearby spindly legged table. As he was plunked down in one of the chairs by Mrs.

Mahogany's pudgy hands, Sadar decided that there wasn't enough room in the entire lobby for Mrs. Mahogany. She needed a nice desert island.

"My dear Mister Sadar, you must tell me all about that exciting flood. It made the most terrible roar all over town. I was talking to old Mister Owens . . . he comes here for his hay fever every year, you know . . . and I was just saying to him. . . ." Not having taken a chair herself, Mrs. Mahogany shuffled, swirled, or jumped with each word she uttered.

Sadar managed an occasional polite—"Is that so?"—during the one-woman show. Rouvière and Ralston strolled by and started up the mahogany stairway, Ralston pausing an instant to bend a bitter look on Sadar. The man was without his gun at the moment, Sadar observed. Or, at least, it wasn't in his hip pocket. Before the finale, Terry and Gary had returned to the desk, their faces indicating a satisfactory exchange of coin had been made.

Mrs. Mahogany had veered from Mr. Owens's hay fever to the prevalence of ulcers among professional people and had paused only a moment to check her steam gauges, when, in that moment of astounding silence, Terry and Gary sliced in neatly. "There's a gent in the gents' room to see you, Mister Sadar."

Relief washing through his entire body, Sadar rose quickly, murmuring: "Excuse me."

"Oh, wait, you never did tell me how you got out of that terrible mine!" Mrs. Mahogany protested.

Sadar stopped. "We each seized a piece of timber," Sadar said solemnly. "The water took us at fearful speed down the tunnel. There was nothing but a big roar and darkness, a whole lot of darkness. The thumping of our skulls against solid granite sounded like overripe watermelons dropping from trees. Then . . . then . . . I forget . . . everything went black!"

Mrs. Mahogany squealed delightedly. "You know I had a cousin who used to do the most humorous recitations about. . . ."

"This gent's in an awful hurry!" the bellhop warned.

Sadar excused himself again.

Left at the Mahogany post, Gary shouted: "Hey, watermelons don't grow on trees."

When Sadar found the men's lounge empty, he looked questioningly at Terry.

"Didn't you want to get away from her?" the boy asked innocently.

Sadar grinned and produced a dollar. "You'll go far in this business," he said.

"Thanks. Old P.T.F. gives me only half a buck, but I have to rescue him oftener, so I guess that ain't bad."

"I'd give a dollar to the person who can tell me where the wooden Indian that used to be in the lobby is?"

"That crummy thing?" Terry extended his hand, palm up, as he gave Sadar directions on where to find it in the basement.

He followed the lad's directions, using a screen of diners, emerging from the big room on his right, to bypass Mrs. Mahogany, and went through the dining room to access the side entrance to reach the hall beyond. He passed through a dusty storeroom before coming to the head of the wooden stairs. Light sprang on when he turned a switch. But he found it to be rather insufficient once he made it down to the musty basement where sat an antique furnace that surely had never overheated the guests in the old days. Old furniture, trestles, dusty canvas, coils of used wiring, packing cases, and barrels were stacked along both long walls as neatly as the heterogeneous shapes of the items would allow. Just inside the room, in the left-hand corner, long rolls of old rugs with frayed ends leaned against the wall in sagging postures.

Sadar walked to the end of the room where the bellhop had said the wooden Indian was stored. But there was no carved figure. He searched both sides of the room, peering around furniture and behind barrels. Fifteen minutes later he was convinced there was no cigar store Indian in the basement, unless, he thought, it had been sawed into sections and put in packing cases or had been jammed in the corner behind the rugs.

He made his way to the rugs. Just as he reached out to move one of the bundles, an automatic pistol jabbed out from between two gray rolls, looking as venomous as the steady poise of a rattlesnake's head.

"Don't get excited," a voice said.

Chapter Fifteen

LAST WARNING

Sadar held still while he studied the pistol pointed at his chest from between the rolls of rugs. His right arm and shoulder tingled as he set himself for a quick, upsweeping blow that would knock the gun loose from the hand that held it.

"Don't do it!" said the voice behind the weapon. "Don't get excited and tackle these rugs. I bruise easily."

He recognized the voice then. Jackie Rouvière was hiding in that dusty corner. "What the hell?" Sadar whispered.

The pistol disappeared. He heard the girl scraping along the wall, and presently she came out from behind the last roll, carrying the pistol by the barrel. She ran the back of her other hand along her forehead to remove a few strands of cobwebs that had settled there before handing the gun to Sadar. "It needs uncocking or something. I don't remember whether or not I worked that sliding thing on top that pushes a cartridge into the barrel . . . but I don't think I did."

Sadar took the gun, a .32 automatic, still warm from the grip of her hand. The thumb safety was down. He pulled the slide back and saw a cartridge in the chamber. After he slid the magazine out, he ejected the single load and caught it in mid-air. He bounced the cartridge in his hand, not saying a word but watching the girl.

"What do you know?" she said. "It *was* loaded."

They looked at each other quietly in the dim light.

"Oh, don't be so grim and dark-looking," Jackie said. "I wasn't going to shoot anybody. But I didn't want to get punched silly when you pulled those rugs aside and saw someone and started swinging."

"Why were you hiding there?"

"My father happens to own this hotel!" she snapped, then seemed to regret the statement instantly. "I was looking for the same wooden Indian you were."

He glanced at the gun. "Did you think he was going to come to life and go on the warpath?"

"The gun was in case . . . somebody . . . tried to get nasty."

"Who?" Sadar asked.

For an instant the lower half of her face was faintly suggestive of her father's jaw and mouth. "That has nothing to do with you."

"The dummy Indian might."

"I don't think so . . . unless . . . ?" She studied him keenly. "My father *did* let you go, didn't he?"

"He fired me, yes. What about the wooden Indian?"

"It's gone. A day or two before you came, it was here. I know because I saw it."

Sadar digested the information slowly. From the first that Indian business had seemed fantastic, in spite of the fact that Tarwater had introduced it. The whole thing just didn't seem to have any relation to the calaverite, even though here he was trying to decipher the riddle by chasing after the wood sculpture. Besides, it was all he had to work on at the moment. But now, incredible as the whole deal seemed, there must have been sanity in Tarwater's mention of the carved figure. Jackie, too, was after it, and so was someone else, assuming that she thought she needed a gun for someone other than

Sadar. He looked at Jackie's wrists and forearms. It struck him that, for a girl who could kill a deer with an arrow, she had appeared rather helpless and ignorant about a gun. Still, that could be. . . .

"Any idea where the big chief went?" he asked.

She nodded.

"Where?"

"About two thousand miles from here."

"Great," Sadar muttered with exasperation that usually accompanies frustration. "What makes you so sure that the Indian has nothing to do with me . . . unless I'm working for your father?"

"You'll just have to take my word for that," Jackie said. "I assure you that the Indian has nothing at all to do with your blessed calaverite. I'm a little tired of being cross-examined, and of the musty smell in here, so, if you'll just give me back Myra's gun and. . . ."

"I'll carry it up for you." Sadar positioned the weapon in his pocket. "Sim Tarwater feels different about that Indian."

She gave him a startled look. "Sim!"

They heard the stairway door open. The lights went off, then snapped back on, and someone started down the wooden steps.

"I'm going to take Biff-Biff back to Sim tomorrow morning," Jackie said quickly in a low voice. "Will you walk over with me?"

He nodded, just as puzzled as ever when he was around Jackie.

She raised her voice. "Now take this rug right here . . . don't you think it would make a nice floor mat for the jeep?"

"No," Sadar said.

Reeves walked into the room. He was smooth. He did a creditable job of pretending polite surprise, but the tightness of his eyes betrayed some raging suspicion.

"Have you seen our antique furniture, Reeves?" Sadar asked. "Some very fine old antediluvian stuff in here." He took Jackie's arm and started for the stairs. "No? Well, take a look, son. All I ask is that you don't forget the lights. Overhead, you know, old boy."

Reeves said nothing. His face was a little pale.

As the couple passed Reeves, Sadar read from the quietness in the red-bearded man's eyes a hatred deeper and more lasting than any Ralston would ever be able to work up. Sadar knew that, if Jackie hadn't been between the two of them, Reeves would have tried to knock him cold.

Before he followed Jackie up the steps, Sadar paused and looked back. "The light, old boy . . . you won't forget?" He sniffed with grotesque delicacy. "I love the perfume in that oil on your beard."

Reeves's eyes were almost shut. He didn't speak.

Sadar faced the fifth day in Sylvanite with a strange mixture of enthusiasm and doubt. His optimism was inspired by the knowledge that others besides himself were sure the calaverite was still underground. His doubt was based on his experience inside Sylvan Mountain. Looking back, he realized how silly his seven-day proposal must have seemed to Tanner, or to anyone who knew what the inside of a mine looked like after thirty years of abandonment. He realized that, without admitting it, he had known how impossible his pact had been. But he had been fired up, then, with anger and determination. Now only the determination was left.

He tried to ignore all the bothersome side trails that stemmed from the main path, inviting though they were: Jackie's unexplained interest in the wooden figure; Ralston's renewal of his association with Rouvière; Ben's warning to

Sadar, a cautioning against something at which Ben was merely guessing. Perhaps all these branching paths led to the main trail, instead of from it, and, once all the facts were known, he would find all side paths contributing to the final answer as tributaries spend themselves to make a river. The strongest lead he had—and it was dead ahead on the main line—was Tarwater's jumbled story.

Now, as he stood in the early morning sunlight in front of the Big Stope Hotel, looking at Sylvan Mountain, he wondered if he had made a mistake in not waiting for Tarwater's return yesterday, in not having attempted to pin him down and make him talk coherently. This time, when he went, perhaps it would best if he stayed on Tarwater's heels until the former Vivandière shifter made sense, even if he had to wait until after dark when Chinook might be prowling around outside. Besides, this time he would be going with Jackie.

Sadar stood looking up at the pink waste piles fanning out from the Hibernian portals. It was early. His appointment with Jackie was three hours off. His eyes looked up at the dead lamps hanging on the wagon wheel suspended from the marquee. An idea crossed his mind, and he went back inside the hotel. His idea paid off; he found carbide for lamps in a mop closet off the kitchen. He retrieved one of the lamps from the wagon wheel by resting one foot on a windowsill and springing out to do his unhooking in mid-air. Unbeknownst to Sadar, two passersby out for an early morning walk observed his feat with mingled admiration and curiosity.

Lamp in hand, Sadar began to make his way toward the dump of Hibernian Number Six. He passed Ducray's shack, where he observed the old man standing in his garden. They exchanged waves.

At the site, Sadar entered Number Six through its half-open door. Four hundred feet inside, he began to encounter huge sloughs from the roof, cave-ins that had left overhead gloom above the range of his light. He climbed over piles of muck, cursing the numbness setting into his feet and legs as the cold water in the pools through which he had to wade soaked through his shoes and pants and seemed to clamp, vise-like, at his bones.

Soon he reached timber, posts that were askew, water-soaked caps that still held ends of sagged lagging. He paused only briefly and then walked on, careful to avoid touching the timber. Scattered about posts that no longer held up anything leaned against the walls like frozen corpses draped in sheets of ghostly white mold. The air was dead and thick. Only he, the lamp, and the water that managed somehow to work its way out were alive. Where timber had slipped from time-slaked hitches, he knew the ground above was probably sound. Where posts and caps still stood in position, he knew that only incredible weight was holding them that way.

He went on, scrambling over muck piles, twisting and contorting, all in an effort to avoid contact with timber just leaning harmlessly. Then he came to a place where he could go no farther.

He returned to sunlight, realizing Number Six was no good. He sat down. Sunshine warmed his upper parts quickly, worked its alchemy more slowly on his wet legs and feet. He looked farther up the mountain. Sadar knew that the Vivandière vug had been on level Four, and that the levels of the two mines rose almost exactly at the same stages. If the thieves had lacked time to move the sacks of calaverite, he was certain they couldn't have gone much farther than one level up or down from Four in either mine.

He headed toward Five Hibernian, down at the portal. He passed it without going near the dump and continued on up to Four. There was no travesty of a door on the entrance, but Ralston's warning notice was fixed clearly there. Sadar ignored it.

Less than a hundred feet from daylight he encountered timber that was a worse jumble than he had found in Six. Although less than seven hundred feet along the mountain from the Vivandière tunnels, the Hibernian bores had been driven in a loose intrusion of quartzite that required plenty of timbering. He made another hundred feet before admitting that to go farther was worse folly than had been entering in the first place.

No believer in prescience, Sadar couldn't say what made him turn suddenly in the act of shutting off his lamp once he reached daylight. But there was Jack Ralston, his face damply pale, standing above the portal. The automatic he held was rock-steady.

"I warned you, Sadar!"

Sadar was deliberate in his actions, ignoring Ralston and giving attention to his lamp. He finished closing the water valve. When he looked back at Ralston, he realized he had made a mistake. All the man's anger was concentrated in his face. The gun was a bluff.

"What damage do you possibly think I could do to your mine?" Sadar asked. "And, for your information, I'm not scouting for Rouvière, either. Besides, he must have told you last night that he fired me."

"You trespassed after I warned you."

Sadar detected a rising intensity in Ralston's voice, a tremor in the hand that held the gun. But he ignored these little warnings, and he laughed. "So I did, Ralston."

He saw the muscles around Ralston's mouth contort. The man's face darkened. His eyes went wide as if he were losing control of himself.

"You saw my sign and trespassed!" Ralston shouted.

Sadar was motionless. He realized with a stomach-twisting shock that he had gone too far, that he should have crawled, shown fear, and let Ralston curse him and threaten him until his fury had passed. Now Ralston's temper was on the point of erupting from the muzzle of that automatic in a frenzy that might not be sated until the gun was empty. Quickly he estimated the distance to the portal. If he could leap back to safety, let Ralston's poisonous fury dissipate itself through words instead of through the gun. . . .

When he thought about it afterward, Sadar knew he must have done a creditable job of concealing his surprise, although his recollection of the happenings raced through him like a chill now. As he was considering the possibility of jumping clear of harm's way, Deedee Ducray had slipped out of the trees and crept carefully toward Ralston. He held his big hands before him poised like a wrestler. He was soundless without his shoes. The smooth cap of his gray hair was bright in the sunshine.

"I'm sorry, Ralston . . . ," Sadar said, trying to hold Ralston's attention, assure him, assuage his anger.

Ralston's thinking was guided by his growing fury, however. His lips twisted, and he raised the pistol a trifle.

Sadar read death in Ralston's actions. He leaped for the portal.

Then—"Jack." Ducray's voice was barely raised above a whisper. And Ralston whirled straight into Ducray's big, waiting hands.

Sadar heard the struggle before he had risen from his hands and knees near the portal. He ran up the hillside in time to see the pistol drop to the ground, in time to see that Ralston's struggles were like the writhing of a crippled ant under Ducray's deft handling.

"Don't hurt him!" Ducray grunted as Sadar leaped in to assist.

Sadar was surprised to find that Ralston was equipped with incredible stores of strength. But then suddenly it seemed to leave Ralston, like air escaping from a balloon.

As they lowered Ralston to the ground, Sadar noted the foam around his lips—that his eyes were open, but they didn't see—that his jaw was jerking, and one side of his face seemed lower than the other.

Breathing hard, Ducray pulled a handkerchief from his overalls' pocket and began dabbing at Ralston's right wrist where the flesh had been twisted away. "You shouldn't have got him so sore!" he accused.

Sadar looked at Ralston's contorted face. "I know it, now."

"I guess I should have told you. He had Saint Vitus's dance when he was little, and the other kids used to tease him something awful just to see him throw a fit. That's why he can't stand to have anyone laugh at him or cross him . . . even about some little stinking thing that don't matter."

Sadar felt ashamed as he looked at the thin-shouldered man on the ground. He recalled the pitiful defiance that had underlain Ralston's anger the night the beefy lad had come at him in the Windlass Bucket. Then he remembered his own tormented boyhood—but *he* had been strong and capable of fighting back.

"I'm sorry about this . . . I didn't know," Sadar words came tripping out of his mouth.

"I should have told you," Ducray repeated. His eyes were tired, and the bony structure of his chin and cheek bones was more prominent than Sadar had ever seen. "You know I seen you go up the hill. Then Jack come along after. You'd been gone a while. I tried to distract him by inviting him in for coffee, tried to talk him out of trailing after you, but he wouldn't listen. So I just sneaked along to see what I could do."

"Thanks, Deedee."

"I didn't want to see either of you get hurt." There was no denying the sincerity of the old man's voice.

Slowly color was coming back to Ralston's face. His eyes were closed now, and he tried feebly to clear his throat.

"He'll be all right," Ducray assured Sadar. "But maybe you'd better not be around when he comes to." He nodded back toward the trees above the tunnel. "But would you get my shoes for me before you go?"

Having retrieved them, Sadar noticed the old man's shoes were just about worn out.

Chapter Sixteen

A JOURNEY INTO THE PAST

Back at the hotel, Sadar hung the lamp on the wagon wheel with another side leap from the purchase of the nearby windowsill. Upon his entry, guests, lulling about in the lobby, stared critically at his muddy, disheveled appearance. He explained his condition to Mrs. Mahogany as being the result of a ride on an inner tube through the cañon of the Tumbling River, knowing the story would reach all within earshot before he had time to attain his room and change his clothes.

In a half hour's time he and Jackie were headed up the mountain with Biff-Biff. The playful bear cub persistently tried to pass on the wrong side of trees, tangle his chain around rocks and stumps, or sit down stubbornly in the middle of the bridle path when all other devilment failed to get attention.

"Maybe Dad was right . . . we should have used the jeep to take Biff-Biff back to Sim," Jackie said. "You know, I wouldn't be surprised if he meets us by Sim's so that he can take us back."

"He doesn't trust me, then?"

Jackie paused to unhook Biff-Biff's chain from a fallen branch before speaking. "As far as the calaverite goes, he thinks you're a bad influence on Sylvanite. His attitude toward you personally is something I don't pretend to know. He generally knows what's going on, but he always makes sure before he acts."

"What does that mean exactly?" Sadar asked.

"A lot of things that you wouldn't be much interested in . . . a few things connected with the wooden Indian."

"I *am* interested in that wooden Indian. Sim was on the verge of telling me more about it, if you recall, when you and your father scared him away."

Jackie frowned and shook her head. "You must have misunderstood him." She seemed to be lost in thought for a couple seconds. "My gosh! You don't suppose that dummy *did* have something to do with the calaverite?"

Sadar gave her a dark look. "I wonder?"

They walked on in silence.

"Of course, if it does, it isn't important," Sadar said. "Just a hundred thousand or so in gold . . . money that goes smack into your old man's pocket, minus ninety-nine percent for Uncle Sam, of course."

"You sound a little bitter about that gold."

"I am . . . and I'll continue to be, if it's never found." He switched his attention from the trail to her face for several moments, then began to tell the story of his life and why he needed to find the twenty-seven sacks. "The more I see of bitterness stemming from that vug robbery, the more determined I am to find the gold and shake myself free of the curse of the whole thing. I may go broke trying. I may have to try to lease the Hibernian and the Vivandière and start from scratch, but I'm going to keep trying."

She nodded, stopping in the middle of the trail they were following. "I suspected something of your feelings, when I made that crack about your grandfather the other day." Tears suddenly and unexpectedly filled her eyes. "I'm really very sorry for having said that. I guess I have a bad habit of saying the wrong thing."

"Wait"—Sadar reached out a hand to reassure her, touching her shoulder gently—"it's OK. I really didn't mean to make *you* feel bad." He was more confused than ever about this mysterious girl who seemed cocksure so much of the time, yet now appeared so vulnerable.

"It's not anything you said," Jackie replied, stepping back, her shoulders sagging. "It's this town . . . these mines. . . ." She turned, raking her fingers through her hair. "This place killed my mother and my brother. You couldn't know that . . . and you don't understand. Out of respect for my father . . . and, I guess, for me . . . everyone here has taken a vow of silence on the subject. So it's like my mother and Jimmy never existed. And over the years, little by little, the silence has been eating away at me. With all the recent talk of searching for the calaverite again, I've been reminded of Mom's fear of the mines. A fear that turned out to be all too real . . . when Jimmy . . . when Jimmy. . . ." She couldn't go on. It was too hard.

Sadar encircled Jackie's trembling shoulders with his arm and steered her toward a group of rocks a short distance from the trail. Once she was seated and somewhat calmed down, he said: "You don't have to talk about this. It's really none. . . ."

Jackie's hand gripped at his shirt sleeve, as she pleaded: "Don't you see? *I* want to talk about it. I *have* to. That *not* talking about it is worse than talking about it. I drink just so I don't talk about it . . . don't think about it. But I can't go on pretending I didn't have a mother and a brother."

"It's all right, Jackie." Sadar tried to comfort her, but he now felt even more strongly that this was none of his business. "Isn't there anyone you can talk to about this?"

"No, there's no one, and, if I did and Father found out . . . ,"—she paused to wipe her nose on her shirt—"I don't know. So the answer is no . . . no one. When you told me about your own past, I thought you would understand. I'm sorry." She muttered these last words, and began to stand up, adding: "I shouldn't burden you. . . ."

"Wait, Jackie," Sadar insisted, standing up to pull her back onto the rock. "I'm the one who should be sorry. I'll listen, if you want to talk."

"My mother, Rose, was from Connecticut," Jackie began as she eased herself down on the rock. "Her family was well-connected. She met my father in New York while on vacation. He was working on a big real estate sale, at the time. It was a whirlwind courtship from what I gathered from things my mother said when she was alive. Anyway, they married, moved West, and settled in Sylvanite because of the mine and land Dad had inherited. Father built a beautiful home . . . I guess you'd call it a mansion . . . on the other side of town"—she pointed in the opposite direction.

"But there's no mansion over there," Sadar inserted, scanning the hills to the south. "There's not a single house. . . ."

"I'll get to that," Jackie responded. "So, Mother lived in this lovely home set apart from everyone else, alone most of the time. She wasn't a snob, you understand . . . just embarrassed to go into town where she was viewed as odd because she was educated and used proper English. God, her manners were impeccable. So, Sylvanites kept their distance, and so did she. That changed a little when Jimmy was born. A few of the women, including Prudence Wright . . . the woman who's always at the hotel. . . ."

"Missus Mahogany?" Sadar gasped, and Jackie looked at him nonplused. "I call her that because the first time I encountered her she was carrying on about painted mahogany."

180

"Her name is Prudence Wright. She eventually worked in our house . . . not exactly a servant, rather a companion and helper to Mom. Now Dad pays for a room at the hotel for her. Though, God knows, she's rarely in it. I don't think she even sleeps there most nights. Every year since my mom died, she goes a little more batty. Her husband was killed in a mining accident a long time back. The point is, once Jimmy was born, some things became easier for Mom because of a few women like Prudence, and some things became harder. Once Jimmy was old enough to go to the mines with Dad, then Mom had two people to worry about. And then I was born two years later. I understand she had a difficult time . . . confined in bed and all that . . . so Jimmy was with Dad more, which caused her even more worry.

"Jimmy and I had twelve years of heaven growing up on that hill. We were together all the time. Jimmy could make everything a game. And Mom worried about us every minute of every day. I remember how she would check on us all through the night. First she'd go to Jimmy's room, then mine. She'd open the door, come up to the bed, stand there for five or ten minutes at least five times a night, and, right before she'd leave, she'd stroke my forehead. I guess she just wanted to be assured that we were alive." Jackie paused, staring off into the distance. "Her constant attendance drove Dad crazy, but he couldn't change her thinking.

"Then, when Jimmy was fourteen . . . it was a Tuesday in the middle of June . . . he went with Dad to the Viv. They were re-timbering the entry of one of the levels . . . I forget which. Jimmy wanted to help. Something went wrong . . . one of the supports slipped . . . Jimmy was crushed. Mom's fears were confirmed. After that, she wouldn't let me out of her sight for weeks. She kept vigil at my bedside all night, every night. It seemed she never slept. Then one morning I woke up and the chair where she usually sat at the foot of the bed was empty. Eventually I found her in Jimmy's room, sitting on the floor, holding his pillow in her arms like a baby . . . rocking it. She wouldn't leave the room.

"Prudence and I moved her to her bed, but she just kept going back to Jimmy's room. Dad had given up on her weeks earlier. He kept busy, but I know he blamed himself for what had happened to Jimmy, and then what had happened to Mom. He just couldn't talk about it. Never has. It was about five months after Jimmy's death that Dad had to go out of town on business, and because Mom wasn't paying attention to me any more, he took me along." Jackie stopped short. She stretched her head back and stared blindly into the sky.

Sadar remained silent, cursing himself for his uselessness in this situation.

Still staring blankly, Jackie continued: "Prudence had gone to town to pick up the weekly supplies. Mom was alone. From what we could piece together, she gathered all of Jimmy's belongings and piled them in the center of his room, creating a pyre for herself. Some old man in town saw the flames coming from Jimmy's window on the second floor. He got help, and the fire was stopped before it had spread too far. But Mom was burned horribly, and she died. Dad never said a word. He razed the house to the ground before a week had passed. Except for two small headstones . . . one with the words wife and mother and the other reading son and brother . . . there is no indication that it was once our home." Finished, Jackie shifted her gaze to Sadar, and, nodding her head, she repeated the words—"our home."

"I'm glad you told me," Sadar said finally. "We're sure a sorry pair, aren't we?"

"Yeah, prisoners of that damn' mine's past," Jackie

agreed, a weak smile twisting at the corners of her mouth. "Thanks for listening."

"I'd say that's a powerful lot of story to keep bottled up inside. You sure you can't talk to your father about this?"

"I'm afraid to, Rigdon. Just a chicken."

"You know, it might do you both good to try," he suggested, relieved at finally having the answers to the many questions that had surrounded Jackie Rouvière.

"Now, how about telling me what prompted you into walking over here with me," Sadar asked.

"I guess I wanted to find out what you've told me about your connection with Sylvan Mountain. Maybe I can help, if I give you some of the facts that Dad's uncle passed on to him about that robbery."

"One of the first things I'm trying to figure out is how this Indian fits in with the whole thing."

Jackie shook her head. "I'm sure it has nothing to do with the calaverite, even if Sim did mention it to you. When we get over there, we'll let him tell us."

"All right. Then, tell me what Ralston's cooking up with your father."

"I'm not sure, but I think it's the same old deal about the Hibernian. Since you came to Sylvan, Ralston seems more convinced than ever that the calaverite is in a little cross-cut or drift or something way back on the fourth level. His reasons, Dad says, are not very sound, but Dad doesn't want to offend him again by turning him down just as he did last time. Ralston just about went crazy back then. He was ready to beat Dad to death with a telephone."

"I know all about his temper," Sadar assured her. "As a matter or fact, I misjudged it this morning." He told her about what had happened earlier in the day.

As Jackie stood with her mouth open, Biff-Biff surged

ahead, apparently having decided to be the dragger instead of the draggee. Together, the two restored order with a bit of coaxing at the chain that secured Biff-Biff. Puffing from the exertion, Jackie commented: "That's Deedee for you. He's always trying to help out some poor devil."

"How much do you know about the inside of the mines?" Sadar asked, wanting to get back to the subject of the robbery.

"Nothing about Ralston's Hibernian. In fact, there aren't any maps of it any more. Ralston's father had them, and he looked for the calaverite for years without any luck. He used up what little money Jack's grandfather had left after some bad investments swallowed up most of the Hibe's profits. After Jack's father struck out, a few others leased the mine and gave it a try. Eventually three men were killed when they started to take out a few old timbers to look behind some lagging. Jack's father tore the maps up, then and there, and swore he'd never have another thing to do with looking for the gold, nor would he let anyone else."

Nothing but violence had come from the calaverite, Sadar reflected. *Nothing but bloodshed and bitterness had come from twenty-seven sacks of high grade that were only briefly in anyone's actual possession.*

"What do you know about the Vivandière?" Sadar pursued.

"I've gone over the level charts with Dad, and all the records and personal observations Marcus Besse made about the robbery."

"Tell me, then, that bulkheaded place on Two . . . the place where the engine crashed through on its way to the bottom of the stope . . . how tight was that at the time of the robbery?"

"Like a drum. Marcus Besse's records show that the stope

was blocked with four-inch planks from wall to wall. The opening that came up from Number Three had been blocked by cave-ins and bulkheaded off. Dad's uncle had a brother-in-law, a big fat Frenchman who was a shift boss on Number Two. He spent most of his time sitting in a little shack right on top of the bulkhead. Besse's records show that his brother-in-law spent his whole shift smack-dab in that one place the night the vug was robbed. There were trammers, tool nippers, and others going back and forth all the time."

That would eliminate the theory that the thieves had somehow gotten into the old stope where the engine was, Sadar thought. *Well . . . it had been only an idea.* It struck him that those who had searched the mountain forty-five years before had had knowledge far beyond what was remembered or available now. *But they must have missed something, or maybe somebody had found the ore and gotten away with it during the search.*

"Did the Vivandière operate full blast right after the robbery?" he asked.

"Both the Viv and the Hibe shut down for a week. Marcus Besse, Theodore Ralston . . . that was Jack's grandfather . . . your grandfather, Sim, and a few other men Besse trusted searched and dug and prodded and did everything they could think of to find out where the sacks had gone. Then Ralston protested about the loss of time, even though Besse was paying all the expenses incurred by the delay, and so both mines re-opened. But they still kept looking."

Sadar gave Biff-Biff a gentle nudge with his foot to get him to move ahead. "You make it sound hopeless."

"If you'd gone over the records, you'd say so, too." Jackie paused to fling a stone down the hill like a boy. "My Dad chewed over every bit of information there was and decided, finally, that the possibility of the ore still being underground or of its being recovered, if it was, were so poor the whole deal was a bad investment."

Sadar stripped a twig from an aspen and chewed on the bitter leaves. "Somebody besides me doesn't think so."

"The person who tried to trap you for good in the Commander?" she asked quietly. "I have eyes, too," she added when Sadar stared.

He nodded. "Or the person who . . ."—he looked at her wrists and hands, remembering that she could draw a bow to kill a buck deer—"who tried to put a broad-head arrow through me the first night I was in Sylvanite."

She stopped in the trail. Her eyes went wide, so wide they looked more like her father's than ever. "Not true, is it?" Jackie said.

"Oh, yes." He told her only scant facts about the incident.

She shook her head soberly. "This is getting to sound like a nasty affair."

As they walked on, Sadar decided that the hoof marks he had been studying in the trail for some time were quite fresh. He unwound Biff-Biff's chain from around a tree. They climbed toward Sim Tarwater's cabin in silence.

A horse, tied well off the trail in the timber that edged the cabin, had been watching them for some time before they saw it. The owner of the horse, standing behind a tree with a rifle and looking toward the cabin, didn't see or hear them until they were quite close. It was Reeves, and he swung around quickly when Biff-Biff bounded toward him, Sadar having let loose of the chain. Reeves stooped and played with the cub for a moment, straightening with a smile, a smile that was intended for Jackie only. He didn't seem to see Sadar.

"I didn't have enough force to leave a rear guard," Reeves said easily.

"What's this Daniel Boone business about?" Jackie asked.

"Oh, I've sort of been irked lately about the way your father has been riding me about those wandering steers on the ranch. Some of them, I've determined, wander clean down to the Fire Horse Club and get passed out on a plate to those old coots . . . or anyone else who hangs out there." He still hadn't acknowledged Sadar.

"If you want to make a crack about me, Reeves, speak right up!" Sadar said.

"I'd suggest both of you pull back your horns," Jackie said calmly. She smiled at Reeves. "Has it taken you all this time to suspect where those steaks at the Fire Horse come from?"

Reeves flushed a little at the implication. "You aren't saying . . . ? Why didn't you say something?"

"What you and Dad didn't know helped give those old boys a square meal once in a while. Don't worry about it too much, Biff. It didn't come out of your paycheck. Besides, I've talked Dad into giving me the stock on the ranch. So, they're my cattle. Let me handle the critters and Dad."

Reeves's face showed all the chagrin of false importance, having discovered information that had been withheld from him. Smiling to himself, Sadar's opinion of Jackie was growing by leaps and bounds this day. Nonetheless, Reeves recovered quickly and shrugged with a tight smile, while the sharp flick of a glance at Sadar displayed his bitterness at having had a witness to his stupidity. "Somebody should tell me these things," Reeves finally said. "Perhaps I'd better ride on up and apologize to Sim." He had a little trouble holding his sarcasm below the grating point.

Sadar looked thoughtfully toward the cabin. No wonder Tarwater had been nervous the day before when Jackie and her father had stopped to ask if he'd seen any stray steers. Sim's hasty departure may have been directed at burying a hide or dumping offal down a prospect hole.

"How'd you find out Sim was giving your steers the old Robin Hood treatment?" he asked the girl, as he headed toward his horse.

"Ben Liggett. He was worried and offered to go to work for Dad in order to pay for the steers, if I'd not say anything about Sim. Ben thinks a lot of his old friends, you know," she said, then added as she walked on toward the cabin: "That's a trait I admire in a man."

No smoke showed from the pipe sticking out of the roof. At sight of the visitors, the two conies scrambled into their refuge, and several chipmunks scattered in alarm. Sadar expected the door to pop open long before he was near enough to knock. He was surprised when it did not, so he rapped. He was about to knock again, when his eye caught the glint of bright steel in the end of the little passage that served as a man-way for Sim's small pets. He moved in for a closer look. Three stiff-backed, single-edged razor blades had been forced into the end of the narrow board that formed the bottom of the passage. They had been cocked at an angle so that their corners struck above the floor of the exit. Two of them looked rusty. Brown stains formed streaks along the bottom board and on the sides of the square opening.

Biff-Biff whimpered at Sadar's ankles as he examined the opening. Sadar handed the cub's chain to Jackie, remaining silent as his heart began to pound. From the edge of the trees he heard the sounds of Reeves's horse.

Moving down the side of the cabin, Sadar put his hands at the sides of his face and pressed closely to a window. He peered for several moments, squinting his eyes. Then he looked soberly at Jackie and said: "Take the bear for a walk down by the river."

For just a breath her mouth and jaw resembled that of the

elder Rouvière. "What is it? What's wrong?" she asked.

"From what I can tell, I'd say both Sim and Chinook are dead."

He walked back to the door and started to lift the outside bar. It was jammed in its catch by a tiny wooden wedge. He saw that the latchstring had been cut just above where it should have been attached to the bar. He stepped back and kicked upward at the door. The tiny wedge shot up and fell to the ground.

Standing clear, Jackie unstrapped Biff-Biff's collar.

"Where's Reeves?" Sadar asked.

"He went toward the garage . . . to tie his horse, I think."

Sadar nodded, pushed the door open, and walked inside.

Sim Tarwater lay in his bunk, his face leaden, his features ghastly gray and sharp. Lying higher than the rest of his body on a crest of twisted, disordered blankets, his right hand looked like an enormous chunk of raw meat peeking out from a makeshift bandage.

Sadar crossed the room quickly, glancing briefly at the long, rigid body of Chinook on its side across the overturned table. Part of the lion's gums and white teeth showed around its blood-stained muzzle. Heavy-bodied flies rose like miniature vultures from the dark blood matting the animal's hide and forming a little reservoir in an indentation where the floor had warped.

Reeves came in just as Sadar had begun to unwind the cloth Tarwater had used to wrap around his injured hand. The big, red-bearded man took Tarwater's other wrist in his hand and, after several seconds, nodded at Sadar. "He's still alive." He looked at Tarwater's damaged hand as the last of the bloody wrap unfolded. "Great Jesus!" he hissed.

There wasn't much left of Tarwater's right hand. A tourniquet of cloth above the wrist, tightened with the stem of a corncob pipe that was enameled with blood, indicated how Tarwater had survived thus far.

As the two men stared speechless at the mangled hand, Jackie approached the bed, carrying a towel from the washstand near the door. Sadar glanced up in time to see the color drain out of her face. He heard a gasp escape her lips. Then, steeling herself, she began assessing the situation by examining Tarwater's injured arm above the elbow. "He must have loosened that tourniquet once in a while," she said. "But we'd better let it out a little before we tighten it up again and move him."

Meanwhile, Reeves had busied himself with Tarwater's other injuries—several furrows in the chest and shoulder area and two long gashes beneath the rent cloth of Tarwater's left pants leg.

Sadar thought he seemed to be taking a lot of time, and he said so.

Reeves's responded with a sharp glance, and his voice was crisp when he said: "If he's got any deep wounds besides that hand, we don't want them to start bleeding heavily when we try to get him to the hospital."

"That's right," Jackie agreed. "Now, I need to wrap up his hand. Rigdon, find me something clean to use."

Sadar was glad to leave the actual ministrations to Jackie and Reeves, both of whom seemed better qualified than he. He looked around the room, espied a pile of dish towels sitting on a shelf, and got them for Jackie. Once again he studied the room. The table and one chair were overturned. Aside from that there was little disorder. Tarwater's struggle with the lion apparently had been terrible and close and quick. A broad-bladed skinning knife lay half concealed by Chinook's hind legs. The coppery little man had taken a horrible mauling in fending off that blunt, snarling head long enough to send that knife home. Chills tingled down Sadar's spine when he guessed the truth—Tarwater had jammed his right hand into the brute's mouth while wielding the skinning knife.

At the same time all three heard the sound of an approaching automobile from across the river. Jackie ran to the doorway and looked out. "It's Dad!" she shouted, relief obvious in her voice.

At the bed, Reeves straightened, saying: "The hand's the worst, I think. We'll have to try to get him to the hospital."

Chapter Seventeen

DANGER LIST

An hour later Sadar stood in the doorway, trying to figure it all out. He'd been trying all the while he'd buried the lion, swabbed out the cabin, sloshed Tarwater's blankets in the river, and hung them out to dry. The explanation Reeves had given for having been watching the cabin had been reasonable enough. And then there had been Rouvière's fortuitous arrival in his red jeep that had been predicted by Jackie on the way up. But he was most bothered by the fact that either Reeves or Jackie had removed the razor blades from the end of the little pass-through. One of them had done it while he had been inside the cabin. A new thought struck him. Rouvière might have taken them.

Sadar looked at the two objects in his hand: a smoothly cut cedar wedge no larger than a small match folder and a length of severed latchstring that he'd picked up off the floor just inside the doorway. Someone had worked a plan so coldly diabolical it made him sick.

While Tarwater and the lion were inside the shack, someone had come silently to the cabin door, cut the latchstring, wedged the bar in its catch with the little piece of wood, and fixed the razor blades in the end of the board. Sadar wondered if Tarwater had heard any activity? Certainly Chinook would have. But it had taken only seconds to set the trap. Then, when Tarwater found the latchstring cut, he'd thrust his arm through the passage to lift up the outside bar. The corners of the razor blades had ripped his hand. Instinctively he must have jerked his arm back. Judging from the bloodstains in the passage, he must have tried again to lift the bar, but it had been jammed too cleverly to be lifted by muscles extended awkwardly through that tiny exit. The injuries from the razor cuts had probably not been great. Just enough to send the odor of Tarwater's warm blood through the cabin and tingling into the nostrils of Chinook.

The person who had set that ghastly trap had known Tarwater's habits well and must have been watching the cabin to make sure the lion was inside. The dried lion's blood on the floor indicated that the attack had not occurred this morning. Usually Tarwater didn't keep the lion inside after dark, so that meant the trap could not have been set much beyond late yesterday afternoon, a long time for a man to lie helpless, fighting off a growing stupor while trying to loosen a tourniquet at regular intervals.

Sadar took a last look inside the cabin. The floor was still damp from his swabbing. The mattress was bare except for the salt he'd sprinkled on the bloodstains. On the cold stove sat a blue pot coated with years of soot marks from having been set directly over the flames. Sadar had dumped out the potatoes Tarwater had been boiling. The sunlight danced across the table, flashing golden rays across a small pot of mustard. Added to the usual smells of cedar shavings, varnish, food, and tobacco smoke was the strong, unpleasant odor of blood.

He closed the door, recalling Tarwater's limp body and ashen face when they'd lifted him into the jeep, and he wondered if he'd ever be back to watch the sunlight wash across the clearing. Heading to the shed, Sadar stopped to push

Biff-Biff with his foot in an effort to discourage the cub from trying to dig out the conies from under the cabin. The bear gave up on the rock foundation and moved back several feet where the digging was easier. He looked up at Sadar. Dirt covered his nose and ringed his eyes.

Sadar frowned when he saw how carefully Reeves's horse had been tied to the garage. Perhaps the animal had been giving Reeves trouble after catching the lion scent. After all, even now the horse didn't care for the smell of cat on Sadar, and he tried to bolt down the trail after Sadar mounted.

Sylvanite Memorial Hospital was not what Sadar had expected. It was a small, neat brick building surrounded by lawns and lilac hedges.

He met Ben Liggett and Deedee Ducray on their way out. Both looked gaunt and strained. They stared at him without speaking. Ducray was favoring his game hip, Sadar noticed.

"How is he?" Sadar asked.

Ducray ran one hand over the smooth cap of gray hair. "The doc says he's got a chance, maybe."

"Nobody can see him," Ben grumbled. "He ain't conscious, anyway." Sadar thought he saw hostility in Ben's slate eyes. "I knowed that stinking lion would give him trouble, just like the first one he had."

Sadar studied both faces closely. Both men looked solemn and tired—and distinctly unfriendly, as if they were holding him responsible for Tarwater's condition. They left him standing on the concrete steps. Sadar could tell Ducray was trying hard not to limp. And he watched as Ben's heavy shoulders slumped before he was out of sight.

Inside, an enormous, gray-headed woman at a metal desk looked up from writing. "Yes?"

"I was wondering . . . how is Sim Tarwater?"

"Critical. No visitors." She went back to writing.

Sadar shifted uneasily. Like most normal, healthy individuals he liked nothing about a hospital except the vaguely comfortable knowledge that one was about somewhere in case of an accident or an emergency. At the far end of a small passage he noticed a nurse moving briskly from one door to another. Sadar stared. "Is that Myra?" he wondered aloud.

The big woman at the desk didn't look up, but she replied: "It is."

Sadar quickly retreated. He was less than two blocks from the hospital when Jackie picked him up in the maroon convertible he had last seen before the Fire Horse Club the night of his fight with Biff Reeves.

"We're going to see Rob Winters," she said.

"Who's he?"

"The sheriff. None of us around here is above the law, you know."

He was getting used to her by now, and so he wasn't surprised when she asked: "Did you pick up the little wedge?"

He nodded.

"I've got the razor blades."

That did surprise him. "Why . . . ?" was all he could get out.

"For the same reason you took the wedge, I suppose. I shouldn't have touched the blades, I realize, but I pulled them loose before I thought about it."

"Did Sim say anything on the ride to the hospital?" Sadar asked.

She shook her head and deftly eased the auto's left front wheel clear of a bad chuckhole. "Men who have lost a lot of blood don't say much."

"How do you know?"

"I took aid training at the hospital Myra worked at during the war."

"Does she work at Sylvanite Memorial all the time?"

"No," Jackie responded. "When they need help, they call. Myra goes in a couple times a week. I help out maybe once a month."

An awkward silence filled the car, until Jackie said: "Listen, about our conversation this afternoon. . . ."

"What conversation?" Sadar joked, trying to reassure her. "It's forgotten, unless you ever want to talk again."

Jackie kept her eyes on the road, but Sadar saw a wave of relief work across her face.

The high-ceilinged sheriff's office in the courthouse was dusty and had a sterile smell. The thin, bald-headed, gray-eyed law man named Winters, who sat and listened to their account, seemed to be drowsing. Now and then he raised drooping eyelids to ask a question in a whispery voice, and Sadar read cold intelligence in both his words and the quick flash of his gray eyes.

Winters looked at their exhibits. "I suppose you shouldn't have touched those blades, Jackie . . . and you, Sadar, maybe shouldn't have cleaned up the cabin."

"The flies, and that lion . . . ," Sadar tried to explain.

"I know what you mean," Winters butted in, then changed topics. "You wouldn't know, but your grandfather, Sam Rigdon, gave me the first real fishin' pole I ever had . . . I was nine years old."

Sadar reflected that among the old-timers of Sylvanite he'd never heard anything but respect for his grandfather.

Switching subjects again, Winters's gray eyes darted out from under drooping lids and fixed on Jackie. "Could have been a print on one of them blades, Jackie." He seemed to drowse off, but then he roused again. "But I don't think so. Anybody that had the cold guts to plan and carry out a deal like this. . . ."

Sadar told him about the night attack with the arrow and about the Commander incident.

In the end Winters said: "I'll throw a little study on the matter. In the meantime, don't take any long fishing trips or go visiting in Chicago." For a moment his eyes were wide-open, watching Sadar. "I don't know what Sim told you, but somebody thinks he said too much."

He didn't get up when they left. He seemed to be asleep. *Winters was,* Sadar thought, *a living refutation of the popular belief that thin men are nervous.*

For Sadar the rest of the day and all of the next were complete frustration, beginning in a series of incidents immediately after he and Jackie had told their story to the sheriff. He had gone directly to the Fire Horse Club to see Ben Liggett and force a showdown on Ben's warning. Jammer and several old-timers were sitting in the casino, laughing and drinking straight whisky. Ben was asleep, so deeply unconscious that Sadar had difficulty rousing him, and even then he wasn't sure that Ben was entirely awake. He blinked with sleep-reddened eyes and said: "Sim die?"

"Sim's all right, but what I want to find out. . . ." He realized he was talking to a sleeping man. The brown-faced man was not faking; he was in a deep sleep, his hair startlingly black against the pillow. He cursed savagely when Sadar half roused him again. Then Sadar gave up, and went in search of Ducray, but there was no response when he knocked on the door of the shack.

He went back to the Big Stope to eat and was virtually dragged into a chair at Mrs. Mahogany's table. She increased his feeling of frustration by telling him, among other things, that Reeves had fired Al Harris and the two bellhops. "They were the only ones in the whole staff who had guts enough to stand up to him," she said grimly, and for once Sadar had a liking for the orange-haired lobby octopus. "I heard Terry say . . . he's the one with the biggest freckles . . . that Reeves discharged Al for being too friendly with you, and the boys because one of them told you where to find a wooden Indian. Is that so?"

"I don't know," Sadar said, but he remembered that, just after the bellhop had told him where to find the Indian, he had met Reeves at the door of the men's lounge.

"You may be sure I'm going to protest to Mister Rouvière!" Mrs. Mahogany said

Sadar decided that he'd do the same, and, if Rouvière couldn't see reason, he'd carry the appeal to Jackie, who seemed to know how to handle her father.

I am, Sadar told himself, *causing a lot of trouble, but I can't stop because of that.*

He didn't get to see Rouvière. That evening the new night clerk told him that the millionaire was in conference and was not to be disturbed. The telephone operator had her orders, too. A red-bearded, heavy-set lad, the same one who had wanted to take Ralston apart in the Windlass Bucket, repeated the orders less grammatically when Sadar tried to get inside the millionaire's top-floor suite.

"What's the big deal?" Sadar inquired, offering the sentry a cigarette.

"That louse Ralston is in there," the lad said in disgust.

Ralston certainly was taking up a lot of Rouvière's time, Sadar observed. And, if what Jackie had said about her father was true, for a man who had already made up his mind against a proposition, Rouvière was giving over a lot of time, simply to keep Ralston's uncontrollable temper from exploding.

Sadar went back to the Fire Horse Club. Ben and Ducray, Jammer said, had gone down the river to Jammer's ranch for some late evening fishing. The only bright spot in the whole day came when Sadar caught a brisk young doctor at the hospital and was told that Tarwater had responded favorably to transfusions and was holding his own. The doctor added with an air of mystery that no outsiders except Winters's deputy or those authorized by the sheriff were to be allowed in the room.

Sadar remembered one of Winters's whispery questions: "None of them windows was blocked so Tarwater couldn't see out, was they?" Apparently the sheriff wasn't taking any chances, figuring Tarwater's assailant might try to enter Sim's hospital room to finish the job the lion hadn't been able to do.

Sadar woke to his seventh day with the full knowledge that he had discarded the last trace of hope to find the calaverite during the time allotted in his pact with Tanner. Even if Tarwater recovered, cleared up his puzzling statements, and told who had tried to kill him, there would still be all those weeks of dead work to get to the ore, assuming that Tarwater's guess was accurate in the first place. Before he got out of bed, Sadar went over Tarwater's incoherent revelations. They made no sense, and, even if they did, the Indian, according to Jackie, was two thousand miles away. That was another sticker.

"Damn that Indian! Damn the whole business!" Sadar cursed aloud.

But he felt better after breakfast, even though he was forced to tell Mrs. Mahogany a pack of lies about giving up all pretense of finding the high grade.

He met Jackie in a blue uniform on her way through the

lobby. She had stayed near Tarwater all night. She looked at Sadar with odd hesitancy before asking: "Are you sure Sim didn't have his bow and arrow the first night you saw him?"

Sadar said he was sure. She left him before he could question her as he had wanted concerning her reasons for the query, due to Mrs. Mahogany's insistent presence. A good deal of his vexed feelings came back, and he damned Mrs. Mahogany soundly under his breath, while at the same time wondering if Tarwater had recovered enough to talk and throw the blame on himself for the attempt to kill Sadar. Or had Jackie planted the idea? What the hell *did* she mean?

He went at once to the Fire Horse where he found Jammer asleep in the second bed in Ben's room. The Swede apparently feared no thieves, for the outside door was open and the patched screen door unhooked. Jammer roused easily.

"You're a regular celebrity merchant!" he said, all his good nature glowing in his little eyes the moment he was fully awake.

"Where's Ben?"

Jammer yawned. "Him and Deedee must have stayed at my place down the river." He massaged his stubby hands and examined them as if looking for missing fingers.

"Did Sim Tarwater have his bow and arrows with him when he came here the first night I ever saw you?" Sadar demanded.

Jammer squinted. "Hell, I don't know. If he did, I never saw 'em. You're not working for the cattlemen's association, are you?"

Jackie certainly did get around, Sadar thought to himself. *The Swede knew that Sadar had been informed about Tarwater's cattle stealing.* "You sure you don't remember about the bow and arrows?" Sadar continued to pursue.

"I never saw 'em, if he had 'em." Jammer grinned widely.

"Played any poker lately?"

Sadar grinned back. "Put your toes out from under those covers and I'll stick some lighted matches between them."

The Swede stopped laughing when Sadar reached the door. "The poker festival opens tonight at the hotel. Reeves always brings in some pretty fast card players. Drop by and watch the fun!"

Driving a brand-new blue sedan, Sheriff Winters picked Sadar up a block from the Fire Horse. He parked the car carefully, feeling for the curb as if his tires might be contaminated by even the slightest bump. "If I'd left word at the hotel for you to come over to my office . . . no telling how much buzz a little thing like that might stir up, not that you're not going to find it bad enough anyway."

Sadar twisted in the seat. "How's that?"

"Some of the facts on how Sim got hurt have begun to circulate. It seems that you got Sim to tell you where the calaverite was hid and then tried to get him chawed to pieces by the lion." Winters picked up a tiny black thread off the upholstery and rolled it between his teeth.

Sadar fought off a wave of quick-rising anger. "That's a damned lie. Of course, you know that?" He looked at Winters for confirmation, found the sheriff regarding him keenly from under sleepy eyelids.

"No man is above the law," Winters said. "If you wasn't Sam Rigdon's grandson, I'd be forced to play it safe and hold you on suspicion of covering up evidence when you tidied up that cabin. Some folks might think it's funny you'd do that. I don't. Some folks might think it's funny to trust a man you never seen before because you happened to know his granddad. In this case, I don't."

"Thanks. Did Reeves start those rumors?"

"I didn't say that. Besides, I look to Sim to answer any

questions about who he saw come near that cabin . . . in a day or two. So just take it easy, son."

Winters started the car and inched into the street as if backing into a fearful stream of traffic.

Sadar was almost deaf and blind from anger as the blue sedan rolled down the street. Reeves was the one, he was sure. Reeves had deliberately, vindictively started the lie. All the years of fighting lies came back strongly. He was too angry to consider that he might be jumping to a wrong conclusion.

The sheriff let Sadar out on Main Street. "Take it easy," the law man said. "I see you got a temper like Sam. So, take it easy, but, if you should have to hit someone, don't start trouble on hotel property. Of course, if two fellows happened to get into a brawl in an alley, or off the main drag, say, I don't think the law would give any trouble . . . if it was a fair fight."

It *was* Reeves!

"Nasty rumors sort of make my work harder," the sheriff said. "Now, some are true, like the one last year that hinted the fellow who found the money in Reeves's treasure hunt was an old pal of Reeves's! That was none of my business, of course, but sometimes I don't have too much to do." Winters examined the edge of the car window for signs of wear. "Besides, I never used a cent of the county's money when I proved that rumor for myself, just out of curiosity, mind you. Other than my wife, I reckon you're about the first one I happened to mention that to." The sheriff looked Sadar straight in the eye then drove off.

Sadar watched the blue sedan go toward the courthouse. Winters missed a deep chuckhole with his front wheels, caught it with one hind wheel. The sheriff stopped the car, got out quickly, and began to examine the car for damage.

Sadar went purposefully toward the Big Stope, one thing in mind: to beat hell out of Reeves.

Chapter Eighteen

THE POKER FESTIVAL

The desk clerk informed Sadar that Reeves had not been in the hotel since shortly after breakfast. Mrs. Mahogany amplified by saying Rouvière and Reeves had been at the office behind the hotel all day. At the office, Dill said the millionaire and Reeves were not there now, nor did he know where they were. A chambermaid, cleaning Reeves's quarters in the hotel, got a scared look when she looked into Sadar's face. She said she hadn't seen Mr. Reeves all day.

Sadar's temper cooled gradually, but not his determination.

It was late afternoon when Mrs. Mahogany came out with information she had wangled from somewhere that Reeves and Rouvière had taken a sudden business trip to Eldorado, but were expected back shortly. "There's something brewing around here," she said suspiciously. "The whole staff is acting oddly. There's something I don't know about." That, she implied, was a grievous condition. "But I'll find out!" she added, as sure as sunset.

Sadar spent most of remainder of the day restlessly. He went to the hospital where he found out that Tarwater was "holding his own." He called on Al Harris, who said he wasn't concerned about getting fired, that he'd had enough of Reeves anyway. He went back to the Fire Horse and to Ducray's, only to learn that they were both still gone. Back at the Big Stope, under Mrs. Mahogany's guidance, he went to the second floor and looked at a huge banquet room he hadn't known was in the hotel. It had been converted into a casino. Mrs. Mahogany warned him about bucking the play.

"It's for suckers," she confided. "I'm not against gambling, you understand, particularly if the profits are used in a worthy cause. Money from this is supposed to go to a veterans' organization, and they have nominal sponsorship of the casino. However, Reeves is the actual one in charge. I've seen a game or two in my travels, but I never did see such downright robbery as goes on here. Reeves imports the gamblers. What the dealers don't steal, the boss gambler and Reeves split. They give the veterans' organization just enough to keep them from blowing their . . . from protesting too loudly." She couched a mental lance. "Mister Rouvière has never seen what goes on here," she added.

Sadar knew that eventually Rouvière was going to get an earful. He felt his respect for Mrs. Mahogany increasing. He tried to remember her real name. *White? No. Wright? Prudence Wright, that was it.*

That she hadn't been blowing bubbles was evident later that night when the casino opened to a jam-packed crowd of Western-garbed players. Poker Festival was not altogether an appropriate appellation. Although there were four poker tables going, roulette, faro bank and dice were getting the heavy play.

Forewarned, Sadar observed the remarkable disparity in the number of chips bought and the number cashed. Mrs. Mahogany paused beside him just long enough to comment on that fact. Then she spied Rouvière across the room and cast off. Her progress toward the millionaire didn't seem hurried, but it reminded Sadar of a bulky fullback barreling through the opposition.

Sadar observed Jammer Roos and two of the old-timers from the Fire Horse looking quite natural at one of the poker tables. Jammer was not doing well. One of his confederates was doing quite well, and the other wasn't suffering. On his own deal the Swede plunged against the house, came up with the lowest of three hands. The highest belonged to one of the old-timers who had stayed through three raises with seeming reluctance. The house man eyed the winner quietly.

While Sadar watched, an alert-looking, craggy-faced man in beautifully tailored gray strolled up to the table and took over from the dealer with a courteous smile. The newcomer wasted no glance on the winner. He smiled genially at the source of the mischief, and Jammer grinned back.

Sadar edged closer.

Jammer lost two small pots, grinned, and twisted his loosened tie closer toward one ear. His shirt already looked like a contour map of the Badlands. He opened on his own deal and drew two cards while the house man's cold eyes watched every movement of the broad hands. The two old-timers stayed in, kept raising back and forth with the house man in the middle. Jammer went along, then began to raise himself. His two confederates laid down, and the house man followed with a set smile.

"Openers?" he requested the Swede politely.

Jammer's hand held a pair of jacks. The rest was dead-wood. "Bluffin' seems to be the only way I can win a pot!" the Swede said jovially.

The house man's smile was getting a little set around the edges as well as in the middle.

Sadar grinned. The war chest of the Fire Horse Club would be much heavier after this was over. Jammer and the other old-timers had rehearsed well during those long hours of card playing.

Sadar saw Jackie enter at the far end of the room. Nearby, Mrs. Mahogany had Rouvière's attention and was giving him the promised earful. He was listening, but he broke away abruptly when he saw his daughter. Rouvière went quickly to her, took her arm, and together they left the casino.

Someone pounded on Sadar's back. He looked around to see old Charley, the one-time railroad engineer. Charley was happily drunk and drunkenly happy.

"This is the stuff, young Sam!" He closed one eye wickedly and tilted his head toward his shoulder. "Money on the tables, women laughing, bright things, things a-moving right along!" He wagged his head. "Ain't seen so much excitement since the week after they hit the big stope!"

"The big stope . . . ," Sadar repeated the words slowly as something started to come to the front of his mind.

"Sure the biggest body of ore they ever opened on the hill. Hell!" Charley looked at Sadar with pity as he noted the puzzled stare on his face. "The big stope, I said! The place where I dropped my Six Hundred ingine!"

Charley's words pulled a trigger in Sadar's mind. *Injun went into the Big Stope.* Great God! How he'd misunderstood Tarwater's words. *Ingine in the big stope. Some geezer.* . . . Why, Myra had even mispronounced the word *geyser* for fun, and still he hadn't tumbled. When Charley's Six Hundred had hit the icy water, there must have been a whale of a geyser of steam and water.

Sadar left Charley in the middle of a sentence, hurrying out the door.

In front of the hotel he found Terry and Gary, lounging suspiciously and eyeing the ring of carbide lamps with skullduggery showing plainly on their homely faces.

"What's the pitch, boys?"

They looked at each other and grinned. "Get us down a couple of them lamps and we'll show you," one said. "We're going to use 'em to write on the hotel windows . . . Reeves is a big jerk and an unfair son. . . ."

"A worthy thought, but a little out of place on those front windows."

"Nobody would see it in back!" one of the boys said.

"Besides, that would be misusing hotel property," Sadar said. He put one foot on the windowsill, leaped up and out, and unhooked a lamp. He turned the water off and blew out the flame. "You guys best stay out of trouble. Tomorrow I'll see if I can square the mess I got you into."

He walked away rapidly, lamp in hand.

"He tells *us* not to steal a lamp, Gary!"

That, Sadar decided, would have to be Terry talking.

He saw a light in Ducray's shack as he passed on his way to Sylvan Mountain. Dark as it was, he had been up the hill so many times in the last few days that he moved surely. He was above Number Five Vivandiere when he saw two bobbing pinpoints of light coming toward the mountain from town. That might be Terry and Gary . . . or it might be somebody else.

Whoever or whatever it was that came charging at him from the trees below Number Three Vivandière several minutes later gave plenty of warning. Sadar swung the lamp in a tight arc, shoulder high, and followed with his left hand. But both blows met only night. When he heard the snuffling at his feet and felt the clutch of little paws, he felt as foolish as a man who starts at his own image in a dark mirror.

"Biff-Biff," he said to the cub as he scratched at its neck, "you're liable to get shot doing that sort of thing."

The cub followed him onto the half-displaced dump of

Number Three, his feet padding behind Sadar as he groped his way into the tunnel. Behind him was the dim sky bowl, the lights of the town, the last vestiges of illumination of all kinds that make travel above ground possible on the darkest of nights. Around him, ahead of him was blackness so nearly total he felt he could clutch it in his hands.

He lit the lamp. Biff-Biff fell back on his haunches as the sudden spit of light startled him. For a fleeting moment Sadar thought the cub was going to bolt from the tunnel. He admitted his great relief when the bear pawed at his eyes and elected to stay. Biff-Biff was a living thing, and living things communicate courage to each other by their presence in utter darkness.

Together, they went up the tunnel, lately water-blasted clear of every loose object. A small stream continued to flow now, working its way from side to side on the irregular floor. Plenty of tracks showed in the thin mud coating left by the flood. Some of the curious throng had gone exploring, Sadar decided. As they traveled deeper into the tunnel, the tracks thinned out, although a trail of footprints made by shoes that had gone and come many times was discernable.

Sadar picked up a curled piece of dry bark and stood quietly for several moments, staring into the blackness beyond his lamp. Biff-Biff pressed against his legs.

Somewhere in the bowels of the mountain, ground moved. Tommy-knockers sent their muffled raps. Sadar was not one to be terrified by his own imagination—but here, far from the earth's surface, bottled by darkness and cold damp walls, he thought of the story of Cornish miners who would never go back into the Argonaut Mine after a large number of their crew were killed by cave-ins. "Ain't Tommy-knockers makin' sounds down there no more. It's bloody dead people, groanin' and tryin' to find a way out."

The Tommy-knockers rapped again, their vibrations traveling down the cold walls as water knocks move along pipes. Icy water flowed by with a muted hiss. Biff-Biff whimpered and clutched Sadar's legs.

They went on. It wasn't long before Sadar felt an increased draft that indicated the flood had opened the mountain clear to the surface under the old railroad. The lamp flame trilled and wavered. Far ahead his footsteps echoed with sepulchral *pooms* as their concussions raced toward every open part of the workings.

The gloom and dampness did much to cool down his first flush of sudden realization about Tarwater's meaning. Tarwater hadn't finished his statement. Maybe the engine reference had been only a starting point. Maybe the flood hadn't cleared the rise that led up to the big stope where the locomotive was. It seemed very unlikely that the raise would be clear because timbers would lodge and jam more easily where the full force of the water hadn't been on them.

As they went on, the draft increased, raising a chill on Sadar's back that wasn't all from the cold. He passed the dark blot of the raise where he and Ducray had saved themselves. That would be about a thousand feet in, Sadar figured, with only two or three hundred feet left to where the jam had once been. He stopped suddenly, looking back, wondering about that raise. How far up had it gone? Still, if it led anywhere at all, it would have been explored years ago by countless people in search of the calaverite. Besides, there was no way to reach the ladder now without help.

On the tunnel floor before him he saw a splinter of bright wood. He picked it up and pressed it between his fingers. The wood was moist, but it wasn't damp enough to have been in the mine very long. Biff-Biff crowded between his feet as Sadar stood staring at the moving shadows.

Somewhere far ahead he thought he heard sound. Then the mine was tomb-like except for the splashing of water. Biff-Biff sat shivering against his legs. Sadar glanced back toward the old raise, and his heart bucketed. Floating toward him was a nebulous, twisting shape. For a tiny prick of time his mind stood still. Then he realized it was a long, thin board floating down the water where the stream widened. The momentary shock taught him the folly of standing still while imagination robbed reason. He started up the bore.

A cloud of fine rock sifted down from the familiar raise behind him. He turned so fast Biff-Biff was trampled. In long strides Sadar went back to the foot of the raise.

The man who came sliding down the footwall on a rope was no apparition. It was Ben Liggett, a square battery lamp hooked on the front of his overalls, one hand trying to hold a long-barreled pistol and the rope at the same time. His clothes were muddy, his hat was gone, and his face looked dead white under his coal-black hair.

He lit hard and staggered across the tunnel. The gun exploded, and a bullet ricocheted toward the portal. "Sadar . . . ?" he said as he turned.

Biff-Biff coughed in terror and began to run around in circles.

Five minutes later Sadar stood at the foot of another raise, the shaft that led upward to the big stope. Behind him, Ben lay sprawled, his wrists and ankles secured with his own rawhide shoe laces, and presumably still unconscious if his inert condition was not intentionally misleading.

Piled ahead in the tunnel was a formidable stack of broken timber and big rocks. Some of the wood showed axe and saw marks. Other timbers indicated dynamite had been used ineffectively, taking out pulpy bites without more than shredding the surface. Overhead, none of the original timber remained. The raise looked dangerous from the eroding and loosening effect of water that had funneled down it for years. Sadar's light fell across a ladder at the foot of the raise. Moving closer, the light showed the form of a sprag at the top of the ladder, and then another ladder reaching upward into the blackness. Clearing that raise from the bottom had been a dangerous job, a task that no miner would have attempted for wages.

Sadar knew that beyond his light there must be hanging unscaled slabs and coffin lids that might come down with no more urging than the concussion of a loud voice or light vibration against the walls; rocks that could tear a man off that frail ladder and spray his body through the wet muck like the tissue and blood of a mouse under the stamp of a hob-nailed boot on a gravel walk.

He hooked the lamp in the crotch of his thumb and palm. The forty-five-year-old trail led upward. So upward he went, alone, the cub having deserted him in his scuffle with Ben. Without the division of a man-way and chute the dark rectangular opening looked like a grave. Climbing upward into a grave was better than being lowered the other way, Sadar determined. His sad attempt at humor didn't comfort him much.

He passed sprag after sprag, light timbers placed temporarily for working purposes. Great gaps in the sides of the raise showed where rock had been torn away by the water. Slabs hung so precariously he could have torn them loose with his fingers. Unlike the solid bore of the level below him, this raise had been run in loose formation, granite softened by talc intrusions.

Four ladders were behind him when he came, dripping wet, into the big stope. Overhead was blackness and dripping water. His light seemed a feeble thing. He knew he stood in an immense cavern where walls, now free of the cold water's heavy pressure, might slough rocks as big as the side of a tall church. Square sets filled the stope as far as his puny lamp would let him see. He knew that, having been under water all this time, they should be sound but, still, their placement against the sides of the stope must have suffered.

Before him a two-by-six plank led into gloom. He stood, reluctant to leave the top of the raise and venture outward into those cells of timber. Fifty feet below on the tunnel level, Sadar could hear Biff-Biff making scared, whimpering sounds. He flashed his light around, and then saw a long rope draped across a wet timber.

Sadar went out on the plank. He found another at the end of the first and followed the trail—deeper into a stope filled with water-logged timber placed by men probably now dead—deeper into a mountain that had been waiting for years to clamp this opening shut, wall to wall. He hoped the bulkhead over him on the level above was still in place. But he couldn't see it.

He moved slowly, testing posts with his free hand, putting his feet out cautiously on the plank. Then he came to a place where the timber was no longer standing. It had been sheered, snapped, crushed by something that had made a gigantic hole through the symmetry of the square sets. He saw the engine!

It lay slanting downward on its side in the gloom like the ghostly hulk of a sunken ship that had died by the head. The smashed pilot rested on the floor of the stope. The other end leaned against a ledge. Sand domes and stacks had been sheered off the torn and ripped boiler; on the side he could see that two of the drivers were twisted outward like deformed feet; the main drive rod had been torn loose to rip upward through the auxiliary air tank, giving the curious appearance of a grasshopper's leg. From all the rotting metal came a noisome smell.

The planks led him to a ledge where the upper end rested amidst the remains of the cab. Thick slabs that might have been soft black stone came away in his hands when he touched metal. He flashed his light around. On the ledge farther behind him lay the twisted links of a safety chain still dangling past a broken drawbar.

Tracks in the slime indicated that this was as far as anyone had come. He looked at the doorless firebox. He hung his lamp in a hole where a rivet once had been and got to his knees. The handful of ore he withdrew was mixed with fragments of fire brick. Leaning toward the light, he dug with his thumbnail at the rock. Frustrated with the lack of light, he wiped the piece of rock on his wet shirt and examined it again next to the flame. He took the lamp off the hook and moved it inside the firebox. For the first time since entering the stope the light was sufficient for its purpose. He could see broken, twisted flues and fire brick. He saw fragments of rotted sacks. He saw the calaverite!

Chapter Nineteen

RAINBOW'S END

For several moments he did nothing but stare at that harmless-looking pile of slimed rock there in the cold maw of a locomotive that had gone from life to this damp gloom in one spectacular moment forty-seven years before. Behind that calaverite was a long, bitter, bloody trail. But now it was ended. Not quite, he amended, but it would be when Rouvière had the high grade in his possession on the surface.

He straightened, listening to the endless drip of water from the bulkhead somewhere high above.

"Well, you found it, Sadar!" The voice came out of the gloom behind the tender.

Sadar whirled so fast he rammed his lamp into the soft metal of the boiler. The light went out.

A switch clicked, and a beam cut through the blackness, revealing timbers he hadn't seen. Ducray came walking from behind the tender. He laughed. "Didn't mean to scare hell out of you."

The old man came closer. Sadar tensed himself. Ducray raised one hand and began to tug at something on his hatband. "Here's a gooser," he said.

Sadar took the fine wire without moving his eyes from the man who held the electric lantern. Ducray moved the torch close to Sadar's dead lamp. "Ain't you going to clear it?" the old man asked.

Sadar got the wire started and cleared the burner hole. He relit the lamp. Ducray hung his own on the boiler and leaned against the right side of the battered engine. Even in the artificial light it was plain to see that Ducray was brutally tired.

He should be, Sadar reasoned. *For two nights he and Ben must have knocked themselves out clearing that raise and putting in those sprags.*

"You knew it was here all the time?" Sadar asked.

Ducray's voice was weary. "Ben knew it . . . I mean he was pretty sure. A couple years back Sim talked some when he had a bad fever and pneumonia and Ben was taking care of him." Ducray stared off into the darkness. "How'd you get past Ben?"

"I had to let him have one, right over the heart."

Ducray seemed to slump. "I hate to think of Ben going like that, even if he did try to kill Sim to keep him from talking to you too much. Ben was hell to turn when he got his mind on something, and he'd had it on this high grade ever since Sim talked. This stope had been blocked for years, but Ben knowed that mud and timber in the raise was slipping all the time, just ready to bust loose. It was just a matter of time.

"Then after Rouvière come back and talked some of re-opening the Viv, Ben was scared. When you showed up and started working on Sim, Ben got awful nervous. He'd planned on this for so long . . . figuring on using the money to help the old-timers around Sylvanite." Ducray was so tired, his words came out easily, unthinkingly.

"After I accidentally busted that jam loose, Ben knowed he'd have to move fast before you or someone else got to prowling. He tried to kill Sim the night after the flood, but I didn't guess that until I heard the story tonight, just before we come up here. He'd talked me into going down to Jammer's ranch . . . so's we could sleep without being bothered, he said . . . but now I know it was so I wouldn't hear what really happened to Sim." Ducray swung one hand toward the tender. "I got sacks over there, twenty-seven of 'em. Before morning we'd have had the calaverite lowered and out of here. I can't say that part of it would have troubled me, but the part about Sim was too much. I was just a-setting here in the dark, thinking about it, when I heard the gun go off back there in the tunnel. If you'd gone out without finding the stuff, you'd never known I was here."

Sadar took Ducray's lamp. He saw it had a bull's-eye adjustment. He pushed the lever around until only a narrow beam poured from the lens. It cut the blackness and played along the dark bulkhead high above them—four-inch timber planked on top of closely spaced stulls of Oregon fir fifty feet long. The bulkhead was black and solid-looking, as tight from wall to wall as it had been following the repairs of damage caused by the plummeting engine almost half a century before.

"How did the thieves get in here?" Sadar asked.

"According to Sim's theory, they come down an old, inclined winze from the level above, at the far end of this stope. The top of the winze was set off to one side of the main drift in a big station, of course. Mell's timber station it was, since the winze had been filled for years. But the muck must have been slipping. The Hibe miners who robbed the vug made a deal with Mell, his helper, and another Vivandière miner, a trammer. After the Hibernian men tapped the vug from the old stope side, they took the ore back into the Vivandière through a cross-cut on Number Four, then on up to Three, and finally up another old raise to Two. In the meantime, Mell and his helper had opened up the old winze enough to get through. They must have had it covered with timber . . . with other timber already cut to put in a bulkhead . . . three, four feet from the top. Soon's the calaverite was hid down here . . . it couldn't've took long with eight or nine men working like fiends while the trammers were booming cars along the bulkhead above us . . . Mell and his helper threw the false bottom across the winze. The trammer brought 'em muck, three cars at a clip, I suppose. In no time the winze was filled . . . anyway, it looked like it was. I suppose they spread chips and timber trimmings on top so nobody in the world would've thought the winze wasn't just as solid-full as it was supposed to have been for years.

"Except Sim was a little sharper than most. He got suspicious about that winze when he scraped his toe down some fresh muck. He was headed to tell about it, when he met Sam Rigdon. Sam had just been canned, and Sim's time was waiting for him. That made him sore, naturally. He got a damned sight madder when his brother was killed. Then all the trouble started in earnest. One way or another the thieves got killed.

"Right at first, when Besse was looking hardest for the calaverite, someone suggested trying this stope. The raise we come up a while ago was blocked and bulkheaded on the level below. Only one or two old hands even knew about the old winze . . . you know yourself that maps never do show the whole parts of a workings. Sim looked at that winze, maybe others did, too, but there it was filled up and solid-looking as a church. But in spite of all that, Sim says, they actually did start to tear out some of the decking on the lower bulkhead above us. It was quite a job . . . you know what heavy plank swelled tight from damp and spiked solid would be like. They would've got through it easy enough, but Besse's brother-in-law talked 'em out of it. He'd been sitting his whole shift, the night the vug was robbed, right on that bulk-head, and he said his honor was being questioned and a lot of junk like that. I guess he raised a lot of French hell. Anyway, he talked old Besse out of ripping through the bulkhead. You'll have to admit it did seem silly to break into a place that looked foolproof and had been sealed off for years. So here the calaverite stayed since before you was born."

Sadar nodded slowly. He's been holding the wire he'd used to clean his burner between his front teeth. Now he handed it back to Ducray, and the old man automatically fixed the gooser to his hatband with care.

Around them was gloom, the dangerous weight of a whole mountain. They were standing beside a fortune in long lost ore. Yet neither saw anything incongruous in the meticulous care with which they handled that tiny piece of thin wire.

"Ben warned me to leave, then he tried to kill me with Sim's bow and arrow the first night I was in Sylvanite," Sadar said.

"How do you know it was Ben?" Ducray's eyes were dark blots in the shadows on his face.

"Because I figure Sim left his bow and quiver somewhere around the Fire Horse Club. When Reeves and I got in that fight, Sim left so fast he forgot his equipment. Ben took it and went after me."

Sadar shot the beam of Ducray's lamp toward the bottom of the stope thirty feet below. It glistened on slime left by the water, revealed jumbled piles of black timber, a stream of water running along the sloping bottom. The stench of wood and metal rotting so far from sunlight was powerful.

"Did you see Ben around the club an hour, say, after I left?" Sadar asked.

"Sim always left his bow and arrows at the back door of the casino unless it was raining," Ducray mused. "I don't remember seeing Ben after you left, but I was in bed, and I went to sleep pretty soon after they got me there."

Water dripping from the bulkhead in a hundred places was the only sound for several moments. Unconsciously Sadar was holding the light so that the beam was dead on the interior of the firebox, giving an eerie illusion of fire where fire properly belonged but would never be again.

"There's no reason why Rouvière should have this ore," Ducray said suddenly. "By daylight we can have it out of here and hid."

Sadar shook his head.

"Why not? Rouvière didn't ever believe it could be found. Hell, he wouldn't even try. He's rich and don't need one cent more. We can divide it. I'll take my share and work it off gradually through the mine on top of the hill. I can use the money to do a lot of good for people that ain't benefiting a damn' bit by all this tourist business. I can see to it that nobody goes hungry . . . that kids have decent clothes and medical care when they need it. I can use every damn' cent of it to do good. Why can't gold that's caused nothing but bloodshed and trouble finally be used for good, instead of going into the pockets of people who don't need it?"

The worst part of Ducray's argument, Sadar hated to admit, was its absolute truth.

"Rouvière can use it to build a rock wall behind the hotel, for all I care," Sadar said. "But we're not taking one ounce, one speck."

"You're a fool, Sadar!" Ducray stretched his left arm along the blackness of the boiler. "Who would know? Who's going to stop us?"

"No good, Deedee," Sadar said. He felt no elation now that the calaverite was found; he felt only great heaviness over the blood already spilled because of that harmless-looking pile of rock inside the engine hulk. He hoped he could find a way to avoid further violence before the long trail ended. For the first time he wished he had taken Ben's gun from where it lay trampled in the water on the level below.

"Deedee, you told me everything I wanted to know, but you reversed your part and Ben's. You're the one Sim told about the ore while he was sick . . . you tried to kill me with Sim's bow and arrow . . . God knows, it must have been agony for you to walk that night, but you did . . . you pinned me in the Commander . . . you set the trap for Sim soon after the flood . . . and you forced Ben into this without his knowing that you'd tried to kill Sim or me."

Water dripped from the bulkhead, sloshed down square sets somewhere out in the gloom, and gathered itself into a stream on the stope bottom. A chunk of rock sloughed from a wall with a dull sound.

Ducray stood motionless, looking at Sadar. Then he laughed. Except for an undertone of tension that might have been due to fatigue, the sound was normal. Ducray shifted a little. The rotten iron of the cab deck broke with a crusty sound under one foot and forced his shoe to come down hard against the ledge a few inches below.

"You're Sam all over," Ducray said. "You couldn't fool Sam. For a minute I thought you might have fallen for it, even when I knew better. Tell me . . . how'd you know?"

"Two guesses . . . things that came to me while you were talking. The wedge in Sim's latch was too neat to have been made by anyone around here that I know except you. Then there was the silent way you sneaked up on Ralston. It took a lot of silence to get near Sim's door without him hearing and popping it open. When you sneaked up on Ralston you didn't yell at him, you spoke quietly. Only a man with chilled steel nerves could do that, Deedee. And only a man with no nerves at all could have fixed that deal up for Sim without fumbling."

Ducray nodded. His voice trembled when he asked: "Couldn't you have got by without killing Ben?"

"He isn't dead. He isn't even hurt, Deedee. If Ben had wanted to stop me, he could have shot me cold turkey when I walked under that raise. He knew that when I hit him, but he'd scared me so bad I let him have one before I could stop it."

"You said you let him have one . . . ," Ducray repeated the words slowly. "That fooled me. It used to mean something else in the old days."

"Your goal has been good all this time, Deedee," Sadar said. "It's been hard for me to understand that a man as unselfish as you could be so cold-blooded when someone got in his way. I can forgive you for trying to kill me . . . but not for the way you went for little Sim, poor harmless Sim Tarwater, who thought you. . . ."

"Shut up, damn you! Don't you think that deal gave me the snakes almost! I haven's slept more than one hour since. I walked around and around the cabin all night that morning before you seen me in the garden when you were going to the Hibernian. But hell's fire! When you've got your heart set on something for years and years like I done with this ore . . . when a man comes into this mine every few months, year after year, snapping at his own insides because he has to wait for time and rot to do something he can't do himself . . . when he's going to be stopped at the last minute? When your brain's on fire with only one thought, do you think friends or anything else matter in the long run?"

"You saved my life twice," Sadar said thoughtfully.

"And I tried to kill you. I got nervous when I first saw you, figuring Sam Rigdon might have guessed as close as Sim did . . . or that Sim might have told him. I tried to kill you the first night you were here. Then I pushed the Commander portal in trying to scare you off."

Sadar was standing at the end of the plank that led out on the square sets. He still held both lamps, the flame of his own directed toward Ducray, the long beam of the other still flooding the interior of the firebox.

"The second time I tried to kill you, Sadar, was when I was showing you through the mines. At first, I figured you didn't know nothing. Then you mentioned Jason Mell, and something inside of me began to burn. I started that flood purposely to. . . ."

"Why? . . . great God, Deedee!"

"You think I took a big chance. If I'd realized the first round on that ladder into the old raise was as rotten as it was, maybe I wouldn't have done it. But I figured on unblocking this stope and getting rid of you at the same time. I faked that hip deal, Sadar, and yelled for you to go on. I knew you'd never make it, but I figured my out was the raise. When you come back and honestly thought you were saving me, it took all the heart out of me." The old man's voice was tired and calm. "It took me back fifty years to when I was a kid and your grandfather carried me out of a caving stope when every other man had run and messed his pants. For a minute it seemed it was happening all over again." Ducray stared out into blackness while water dripped and sloshed from far overhead. "Who knows. I might not have made it up that raise alone. As big and young as you are, you needed help."

Ducray wiped the back of his hand across his mouth in a weary gesture. His face was damp and pale. Sadar's light caught the jut of the old man's high-bridged nose, and made hollow sockets of his eyes.

"Sim's going to get well, Sadar. I'll go to him and tell him what I done and beg him to understand. He knows how I've tried to help everybody I could. Sim'll understand, even if he don't forgive me. I'll do that, if you split the calaverite with Ben and me. Nobody in the whole world, outside us four, will know. Sim may hate my guts and never talk to me again, but he won't say a word about what happened."

There was no denying the sincerity of Ducray's proposal. As foully as he'd played the game, he'd done it under the drive of madness that infects minds with a single, cherished purpose.

"No dice," Sadar said with a tinge of regret. "If Sim recovers, I forget everything. You and Rob Winters and Tarwater can settle things." He paused. "The high grade goes to Rouvière."

Ducray said nothing for several moments. Then he spoke quietly. "Ah, well . . . I knowed you were like Sam. . . ." His long arm went down. There was a crunching break, and his hand came back into the light with the long Johnson bar of the engine. He balanced it in both big hands and stepped forward. "I can't be stopped now," he said simply.

Sadar fell back a step on the plank. He put the electric beam in Ducray's eyes.

"I have to do it, young Sam. I have to." There was a pleading note in Ducray's voice that made his words frightening and terrible.

Sadar fell back two more steps. Now both feet were on the plank, and it was thirty feet or more to that jumbled pile of timber in the bottom of the stope. Too late he realized that all Ducray had to do was stoop and give the two-by-six a quick twist. Without shifting the torch from Ducray's face, Sadar flung his heavy carbide lamp with an underarm delivery. The flame shrilled. The lamp spun within inches of Ducray's head. It struck somewhere near the tender and went out.

The old man didn't flinch. He reached the plank and shuffled out straight into the glare of the blinding shaft of light plastered against his face. His eyes were almost closed. His mouth was clamped hard. He held the black lever like a baseball bat and came on.

"Hold it, Deedee! I don't want to shoot you."

Ducray came on.

The plank would not hold two, Sadar knew. He went back as fast as he could until he reached solidity where the plank rested on a cap.

Neither coward nor idiot, Sadar had no wish to close with Ducray until he had to. That iron lever was eaten into a black slab, but it still had weight. Even if he evaded it and got in close, the struggle would pitch them both to the bottom of the stope.

He felt with his foot behind him for the next plank. He couldn't find it, although he knew it was within inches. He kept the light on the white, set face coming toward him and groped with his toes, and still he couldn't find the plank, just as a man paws within inches of a light cord in the dark. Sadar shifted feet and groped with the other one. This time he found the plank on the first try but knocked the end from its meager bearing on the cap. He heard the plank bumping its way down through the disrupted square sets.

Ducray hesitated a moment, sliding one foot carefully ahead. "Kicked the plank loose, did you?" he said.

"I don't want to shoot you, Deedee."

The old man paused. He moved his face from side to side as if to see around the glare that blinded him. "You ain't got a gun."

"Ben's gun, Deedee."

The old man slid his feet and came on.

Sadar put his forefinger near the back of the torch and

snapped the nail against metal. To his own ears the click was much too loud and didn't carry enough sharpness for a gun hammer. But the sound stopped Ducray all the same.

Sadar never forgot the moment. He couldn't see enough of Ducray's eyes to read his expression. But the old man's mouth didn't move. For what seemed an eternity, Ducray was motionless, the blackened bar of iron slanting past his set face. Water dripped and splashed from the bulkhead. "Didn't sound just right to me . . . that click," Ducray said, and started moving again.

Sadar tensed himself to do the last thing he wanted to do: seize the narrow plank and jar Ducray off it. That was all there was left.

Then Ducray made a misstep. Perhaps he put one foot on the edge of the plank and turned his ankle outward. No matter, he lurched for balance, shifting the Johnson bar before him, and for a tick of time Sadar thought the old man would hold his position.

Ducray's lips flew wide over clenched teeth. "My hip!" he groaned. He fell from the plank so quickly that Sadar imagined for an instant that his beam still held that white, contorted face.

Sadar shifted the light toward the bottom of the stope just in time to see Ducray strike a cap halfway down. It took him squarely across the small of the back with the dull, solid thumping sound that the axle of a fast-moving automobile makes when it strikes a rabbit. Ducray whirled off the timber. His head struck the bottom of the stope first and twisted under his body when he came to a final rest.

Somewhere in the blackness a huge slab fell from the wall with a jar that sent an air concussion racing past Sadar. He wondered vaguely why the light didn't flicker. It was still trained on Ducray's body, which didn't move.

★ ★ ★ ★ ★

Biff-Biff was huddled close to Ben when Sadar began to untie the knots. He found he had done a good job, finally cutting the rawhide with a small penknife.

"I didn't aim to blast you when I come out of that raise," were the first words to pass Ben's lips.

"I know, Ben."

"What happened up there?" Ben asked, getting up with an effort.

Sadar told him everything.

Ben kept nodding his head slowly. At the end, his deep voice was hollow. "I was afraid when you first come to Sylvanite. Deedee told me he knew where the calaverite was, but that was all. When he got something in his head, he was hell to turn. It was him that bossed blowing up the thugs years back. He planted the dynamite. But after he pulled you into that raise the day of the flood, I got to wondering if I was wrong about what he might do. I didn't know about that arrow and the business at the Commander, and, if I'd knowed the truth about how Sim got hurt, I'd've been through with the whole thing. I don't deny, though, that just taking the high grade wouldn't have hurt my conscience a damn' bit!"

He looked into the velvety blackness up the bore. All his age showed. His eyes were dark blots, and his jaw hung as if he lacked the energy to close it. "You're sure he's dead?"

Sadar nodded. "I went down to him."

"I'll go up there and stay with him until you bring help. No matter what Deedee did, there wasn't a better partner in the whole world . . . the whole world." Ben's deep voice rolled into darkness and fell to a hoarse whisper.

"You know, you can clear out, and nobody will know you had any part in this . . . can't prove it, I mean." Sadar picked

226

up the wet gun and gave it to Ben.

"I'll go up and stay with him."

On his way out of the tunnel Sadar heard the heavy footsteps of an old man going the other way, going toward a vigil with loyalty.

Biff-Biff had raced out of the bore ahead of Sadar and was waiting on the dump. Sadar breathed the pure air and was grateful for the fresh coldness of the night. He started toward the lights showing on the dump of Hibernian Number Three.

When Sadar arrived at the dump, Ralston, Rouvière, and Jackie were waiting there. He heard Ralston say: "He went up the hill with a lamp, I tell you! I saw him take it from in front of the hotel."

Biff-Biff went bounding into the illumination of two carbide lamps. Ralston jumped sidewise. Rouvière grunted in alarm and said: "Now what in hell is that?"

"It's Biff-Biff!" Jackie's voice carried to Sadar as he made his way toward the trio.

The millionaire's harsh jaw never relaxed all the while he listened to Sadar's story. Midway in the account, Ralston walked off into the night with a curse. He came back a few minutes later, bitter-faced as ever, and apologized to Sadar for having tried to shoot him. The two men shook hands.

"My advice," Sadar told Rouvière, "is to get the stuff out of there tonight. After we get Deedee out, I'll help with the calaverite as far as the tunnel level . . . and then to hell with it."

"Without the ten thousand-dollar reward Marcus Besse offered for its recovery?" Jackie asked. She looked at her father. "You wouldn't go back on your uncle's word, would you, Dad?"

"Who said I intended to?" Rouvière demanded in the manner of a man who has been insulted—or had his thoughts taken from his mind by someone else.

Ten thousand dollars, Sadar considered, would take care of Ben and Sim Tarwater and the Fire Horse Club nicely.

"You know, Mister Rouvière, these mines, here, have caused a lot people pain. And I can't help thinking that sometimes it's best when these sorts of things are brought out in the open . . . so they can finally be put to rest with dignity. I know things will change for me, now that the calaverite has been found and that the lies will finally stop." He looked significantly at the millionaire, who was looking into his daughter's tear-filled eyes. "I see an old friend of mine is missing from the party," Sadar added, changing the subject. "Where's Reeves?"

Rouvière looked from Jackie to Sadar. "Reeves is not with me any more. I suggested he leave town this evening, just before the Poker Festival began. It took me . . . well, Jackie, rather . . . some time to discover definite proof of his mismanagement. . . ."

"You mean downright stealing," Jackie interrupted. "His bookkeeping was rather fancy . . . he used fake invoices and a few other tricks. He even sold the cigar store Indian and pocketed the money. Wooden Indians are a genuine collector's item, you know."

"They are?" Sadar said. He thought a moment. "I'm sorry to see Reeves go. You see I wanted to beat on him a little."

Rouvière's smile winked on and off. "So did I, but I'm not quite as young as you." He cleared his throat. "Speaking privately, I don't think the final tally will show too great a loss. Rather than face a few unpleasant legal proceedings I mentioned to him, Reeves decided to deed me the Windlass Bucket and transfer a rather substantial bank account he had in Eldorado. And, thanks to Prudence Wright, I learned about the crookedness of the Poker Festival. Just before I came up here this evening, I straightened that out. I canceled the contract with those outside gamblers and put a local man in charge, a man who is honest and seems to know a little about games of chance . . . a Mister . . . well, Jammer they call him. But you know, Sadar, I'll still be in need of someone to run the Windlass Bucket. That is, if you have a mind to stay in Sylvanite."

Under cover of petting Biff-Biff, Sadar concealed a huge smile. "I'll have to think on that offer," he said, catching a glimpse of Jackie looking at him.

"Let's start getting that calaverite out of there," Ralston interjected. "I'd like to see it."

"We've been waiting long enough," Rouvière agreed. "I owe you all a debt of gratitude, particularly you, Jackie. I've been meaning to tell you now for years that your mother would be proud of you. I know I am." And bowing at the waist, he addressed the trio: "Shall we recover that damn' calaverite?"